JIG-SAW

Barbara Cartland

Barbara Cartland Ebooks Ltd

ISBNs

978-1-78867-907-7	EPUB
978-1-78867-906-0	PAPERBACK
978-1-78867-905-3	HARDBACK

Book design by M-Y Books
m-ybooks.co.uk

AUDIOBOOKS

Listen to all your favourite Barbara Cartland Audio Books for free on Spotify, just point your phone camera at this code or go to **https://rb.gy/tx6vrl**

CHAPTER I

It was early April, one of those fresh spring days when the air itself seems to glitter in the sunshine. The new green of the trees shines almost transparent, as the sea in the early morning or a Scotch burn trickling over rocks and fells. The slight wind was whispering of adventures. Excitements, sensations – all palpitating to be discovered. There was a poignancy in the atmosphere as a catch of the breath before a tremendously thrilling experience. The dramatic expectancy of a slowly rising curtain.

Paris was hurrying and bustling, repainting and reclothing to celebrate the departure of a severe winter, throwing open her doors and windows to the new visitor with his promise of golden days ahead.

Expectantly she looked to her lovers and children for new ideas, recreated ideals, fresh hopes, revived ambitions, and the conception of a young springlike love that would give birth to a thousand intrigues and romances.

The pedestrians hurrying along the uneven streets, the bargees navigating their unwieldy craft down the river, even the imperious Gendarme seemed to feel a *gaieté de coeur* born with the first glimmerings of a pale sun, appearing as shyly as a young maiden making her début.

In the boulevards the flower-sellers had piled their stalls with yellow-gold daffodils, which grow, the legends tell us, wherever Persephone places her naked feet on her return to Earth from her gloomy subterranean kingdom where we mourn her incarceration during the cold and darkened winter days.

Beyond the *jardin* of Paris – the *Bois*, with its verdant trees and sparkling fountains – stands the quaint hillside village of St. Cloud. It slopes down to the swiftly moving river, which journeys, winding picturesquely, past the Convent du Sacré Coeur. Nuns in their dark dresses, have for generations cast sombre shadows on the grey stone building with its high stained-glass windows and carved traceries. It is surrounded by gardens, paved and beflowered, the long, smooth lawns edged with yew hedges, which hide ancient secrets imperturbably in their dark green depths.

But this century, the courtyards have rung with young laughter and light hurrying feet, too impatient with the spontaneity of youth, which expects an adventure round every corner, to wander slowly, to let life drift aimlessly past or wait quietly for a glory to come. The long rooms filled with eager, sylph-like figures flitting noiselessly in and out, singing and shouting with happy *joie-de-vivre.* The oak stairs, which have known the gentle footfall of a queen, and the stealthy tread of a murderess escaping justice, feel the irresponsible clatter of feet that jump the last three steps. Even the chapel, dim with age, worn by the knees of countless pilgrims, encircled with an atmosphere calm and beautiful from a history of selfless devotion, seems to rejuvenate when filled with restless, immature, young bodies, their high fresh voices chanting ancient creeds and Latin services.

The nuns loved their pupils, girls from thirteen to nineteen years of age, of all nationalities, although English predominated.

"A grave charge, but an inspiring one," as Monsieur le Curé so often told them. "A direct mission from *le bon Dieu.*"

Today was the last day of the Easter term, and a hundred girls packed their boxes in a fever of excitement and anticipation – chattering incoherently, planning excursions, meetings, parties, for the future four weeks of holiday, writing down addresses, arranging reunions, issuing invitations – all with the free, joyous carelessness of untrammelled youth, at present untouched by reality, ideals untarnished.

In a deserted classroom a girl stood gazing intently at a dismantled desk, emptied of its personal acquirements. Roughly carved on the open lid were the letters 'M.V', artistically filled in with gold paint and red ink.

Mona Vivien was strikingly beautiful, after the type beloved of Botticelli. Delicately perfect features surmounted by soft dark hair which, in some lights, held the blue tints so coveted and affected by the heroines of yellow-backed novels. Her eyes were very dark, and, when she was emotionally stirred, seemed fathomless and changeable as an uncharted sea. Extraordinarily graceful, with a habit of natural pose, her slim figure reminded one of the Venetian beauties of the seventeenth century with their inimitable carriage and mobile movements. When her face was in repose she might almost have stepped down from one of the niches in the chapel, leaving behind her halo and stiff robe. A saint, perhaps, until she laughed, when the illusion vanished as two dimples sprang to life in the oval face, twin twinkles shone in her eyes, while a smile hinted of an Earthly sense of humour.

Yet there was a reserve even in her happiness, as though she never came very close to anything. There was a magical barrier built from an imagination that was vivid enough to inspire belief, an experience that had never touched reality and a religion amalgamated with a fairyland of idealism, which found every stone the footprint of immortality and heard in every stream the music of a thousand celestial voices.

Today Mona was pensive. Sadness grappled in her mind with anticipation, for these were the last hours of her life as a chrysalis. Tomorrow, when the school omnibus lumbered noisily towards Paris, the finished butterfly would enter the world to face sun and shower alike, unprotected. Five years ago, as a small, rather shy child of thirteen, she had been brought to the convent – an alien. Now she was leaving it as one of its children, loving it as a second home – in fact, it was far more real to her than any other, for she had not been to England for many years.

Lady Vivien had arranged for Mona to travel in the holidays with a Governess and her old maid Annette. And they had journeyed through many beautiful countrysides – Provence, Normandy, Brittany, the hillside villages of Italy, the grape-growing vineyards of Spain. And generally, Mona spent a week or so with her grandmother, the Countess of Templedon, who had a villa outside Florence. Adoring her granddaughter, she showed her many treasures of Italy. And so was increased in Mona an already largely developed love of the beautiful and of every branch of art. The Countess also taught 'the science of dress' and delighted in helping her grandchild to choose the soft Italian silks and handwoven brocades that became her unusual beauty.

Intelligent and with such an education, Mona was well equipped to enter the world, save that her ideals were bound to suffer. They were too high, too childlike, too pure. She was fostered and nourished in the gentle atmosphere of the convent and the company of those who loved her. Yet in demanding the highest from mankind she would be accorded the utmost of its capability, even though the effort fell pathetically short of the pinnacle of perfection.

Mona shut the desk with a little bang and walked to the window, looking out over the green lawns and playing grounds to where the river ran like a silver thread at the foot of Saint Cloud. She thought of the generations of women who had shut themselves in from the world, seeing only this peacefulness, knowing only the quiet beauty of the works of God. Neither hearing nor feeling the call of the blood, the glory of fame, swift, palpitating happiness, overwhelming love, or the sadness and shame of defeat, agonising bereavement, unrequited and deserted affection.

The scales were evenly balanced, but the world was there to conquer. Why refuse the challenge?

Yet for a moment she shrank from the future. What lay hidden in the years to come? Years like a long white road, winding through many different lands, until it faltered and faded away into the mists of Death – a journey of threescore years and ten, with possibilities that stretched to the tops of high mountains, powerful, magnificent, omnipotent, or sank in degradation to the bogs and swamps that lurk, enticingly green, by the wayside.

The door of the classroom was thrown open and a pretty girl entered in a whirl of haste and noise.

"Mona, darling," she exclaimed, "I've been looking for you everywhere!"

She jumped on to a desk and sat on the top of it, her feet on the seat. Sally Cutts could never occupy a chair like any ordinary person – she was either balanced precariously on the back or using it as a rest from an extraordinary posture on the floor. An American – which her accent proclaimed in spite of the nuns' gentle efforts to efface it – with corn-coloured hair invariably untidy, a tip-tilted nose between the naughtiest green eyes with dark lashes and a rosebud mouth – she was a very fascinating personality.

Sally was always in trouble of some sort, incorrigibly naughty, although no one could be angry with her for long, for she so obviously enjoyed everything so thoroughly and had more high spirits than could be controlled into decorum.

Her people were very rich and spoilt their only child abominably, but Sally's was far too sweet a nature to be really altered by their indulgence.

Unlike in most things, Mona and Sally had struck up a firm friendship and were inseparable. Mona, although by far the quieter of the two, could be led into any prank under Sally's directorship. At the same time, she was the only person who could prevent her friend from breaking all rules and on occasions venturing to extremes in her escapades.

"Sally," Mona interrogated, "are you sorry to be leaving?"

"I am in a way," answered Sally, "but I'm longing to come out and go to balls and parties and have flirtations and beaux. Pop has taken a wonderful house in London for the Season and we'll have a marvellous time, Mona."

"It is different for you, Sally. You see, I haven't seen my mother for two years and then only for an hour or two at the Ritz, with crowds of people there. She is very beautiful, but I'm rather nervous as to whether we shall get on together."

"And your father?" asked Sally.

"I never see him. *Grand-mère* says he is always working so hard. He is in our Parliament, you know, and always looked worried and busy when I was a little girl. He was very good-looking when mother married him but had very little money. Now he has made heaps, although I heard *Grand-mère* say it was all mother's cleverness and push, which I don't quite understand. Anyway, he was made a Knight in the last Honours' List."

"But your mother had a title before?" asked a puzzled Sally.

"Yes, in her own right. You see, Grandfather was an Earl, but Father was only plain Mister. Sally, do you think they will like having me at home?"

"Well, I shouldn't worry too much about that. They will love you soon enough, Mona dear, and I should do what my Momma says and make my own 'hip-hole in the sand'."

"Oh, Sally, talk English!" laughed Mona.

"Well, make your own bed and lie on it. If you wait around for everyone else, you will get nowhere! Besides, you will be a great success, Mona. You are awfully pretty. Pop thinks you just cute with that saintly face."

"Hiding the heart of a devil!" added Mona. "Finish your story, Sally – you know he said that."

"Well," said Sally reluctantly, "he did say he thought some men would find you played the devil with their hearts, although he guessed that, unlike me, you'd try not to! I mean to have a wonderful time and then marry a Duke!"

"Oh, Sally!" reproached Mona, "how terribly American! Besides, it isn't a bit amusing to marry a Duke nowadays –

only a lot of publicity, everyone watching you wherever you go and taking photographs. An ordinary man is far more fun."

"Now that settles it," cried Sally. "You will marry a Duke because you don't want to, and I shall become affianced to a plain mister called Smith or Brown!"

Sally's face was so disconsolate that Mona burst out laughing. Then, picking up some books and papers to be packed, she started to leave the room.

"Come and help me sit on my box, Sally. It will never shut otherwise."

"Right!" said Sally, scrambling to her feet. "See, Mona, you have dropped something."

She picked up a photograph that lay face upwards on the floor. It was an enlarged snapshot of a tall young man in flannels, tennis racket in hand, standing grinning in the sun. Extremely good-looking, he appeared charming, yet somehow the poise of the body or the turn of the head gave the impression that he was aware of his looks. It was an indescribable but unpleasant 'something' that spoilt a delightful 'whole'.

Sally regarded the snapshot with interest.

"My, Mona," she exclaimed, "what a divine young man! Who is he?"

"My brother Charles," answered Mona. "He sent it to me last holidays and I lost it until today when I turned out my desk, or I would have shown it to you before."

"When did you last see him?" asked the ever-inquisitive Sally.

"In Florence a year ago. He came over for the day when I was with *Grand-mère*. He was nice, Sally, but sort of aloof. I'm afraid he had no use for a flapper sister. Anyway, I shall see him again tomorrow and you will meet him soon, so you can judge for yourself. Listen!"

As they paused a bell began to toll.

"Benediction! I had no idea it was so late!"

The two girls ran quickly from the room and down the long cloisters to the chapel, covering their heads with the soft muslin veils provided by the nuns for the purpose. They entered reverently and joined the kneeling figures.

The altar was ablaze with lights, glittering in golden candlesticks. The sacristy lamps shone on the beautiful, coloured statue of the Blessed Virgin which, surrounded by masses of lilies, was thrown startlingly into relief against heavy blue velvet curtains, while the rest of the chapel was almost in darkness. The congregation of nuns and girls knew the service far too well to need books – or light to read them by – so only the chancel glittered with a dark-set brilliance.

Sister Agnes started to play the organ very quietly as the priest entered. The music seemed to mingle with the incense and drift slowly upwards into the deep darkness of the roof. The girls sang the responses, finishing with the most perfect of all thanksgivings, the *Nunc dimittis.*

'My last night,' thought Mona, and she somehow knew that never again would she worship with such unity of thought, such peacefulness of mind, such singleness of purpose untorn by doubt, unshattered by disillusionment.

With a knowledge of the great world outside would come the 'joy of living', the complement and fulfilment of Nature, possibilities at present only half-sensed by an immature imagination. Yet peace and security would be shattered, gone with the protecting hand of the Convent and an outgrown childhood.

Still, beneath all evils loosed at the opening of Pandora's casket, lay the greatest of all antidotes – Hope, which, 'springing eternal in the human breast', will give strength for the subjugation of all difficulties, the defeating of all obstacles. Hope, ever burning, unquenched as the crimson light before the high altar. Mona on her knees with clasped hands, prayed for divine guidance with all the fervour of a rapidly developing temperament that has known no emotion save of religion, the birth of love and passion, pure and unspoiled, opalescent as the first evening star.

The prologue of her life was over – the curtain was rising on the first act.

CHAPTER II

Mona stood bewildered on Victoria Station, lonely in the rushing crowd around her, confused by the scrambling passengers hastening dilatory porters, surprised at their *brusquerie*, until thankfully she recognised Annette, hot and worried, hurrying towards her.

Annette was French only in name. She had applied for the post of lady's maid in the days when French servants were becoming the mode, and she firmly believed that her engagement by Lady Vivien was due to a judicious rechristening of herself. For her Godfather and Godmothers had approved of Eliza as a suitable, if uninspiring label for a decent and self-respecting English girl, while the journey to the Isle of Wight was the longest she had made across water. From the moment Mona was born, Annette became her devoted slave and was later given sole charge of the child while Lady Vivien procured the services of a smarter and more ornamental maid. Delighted with this arrangement, Annette fussed and patted Mona through her babyhood and was broken-hearted when schooldays separated them. She lived for the holidays when they travelled together and she could again spoil 'her baby' who was growing into a beautiful girl, head and shoulders taller than her old nurse.

That schooldays should be over and Mona a grown-up young woman capable of looking after herself, never entered Annette's head. To her, the child who had played at her knee could never alter and would always need her care. "The eyes of Argus", which had guarded Mona from her cradle, would not slacken their vigilance now.

Round-faced, with cheeks like ripened apples and russet-brown hair streaked with grey, she reminded one of a busy little robin. Her look held a welcome that made Mona feel homelike, even in this Babel and hurly-burly.

"Annette dear! I am so glad to see you," she cried, embracing her. "Will you see about my luggage while I say goodbye?"

She turned back to the gentle-faced nun who had travelled in charge of the twenty-odd girls who were coming to London for their holidays.

"Goodbye, Sister Catherine. I hate saying goodbye to you all. Goodbye, Clare and Molly, don't forget to write. Sally darling, I'll ring you up tomorrow morning – Goodbye and bless you all!"

She hurried away to hide the tears in her eyes and found Annette grappling with innumerable boxes. A large car was awaiting them outside the station and, after a little delay, they drove off towards Belgrave Square.

"Dear London," said Mona, "I remember its funny, dingy smell and dirty blue appearance. Oh, look!" She bent forward and watched a small platoon of Scots Guards marching towards Chelsea Barracks. "Lovely red uniforms again instead of dull khaki – and bearskins! They look just like the tin soldiers Charlie played with in the nursery."

"Wait till you see the Life Guards again, Miss," said Annette. "Do you remember how you loved them as a child?"

"With their shiny tin tummies! I adored them. But, Annette, tell me all the news. How is my mother?"

"Her Ladyship is very well," Annette's voice was frigid. She had little affection for the beautiful woman who gave more hours to the preservation of her looks than minutes of thought to the welfare of her children.

"Is she glad I'm coming home?"

"Oh, Miss Mona dear," Annette looked anxiously at the eager young face beside her, "don't expect too much. The only thing Her Ladyship dislikes is having her plans or orders upset. She likes everything to run on greased wheels."

"And I shall be, willingly or unwillingly, a disturbing element."

The first small cloud had appeared on the serenity of Mona's sky, no larger than a man's hand, yet it dimmed a little of the brightness.

But before she had time for further conversation, the car drew up at 134 Belgrave Square and the door was opened by Miles, the old butler, who had been with the Viviens for nearly half a century. In absent-minded moments he still called Sir Bernard Vivien "Master Bernie", as though he were still the escapading schoolboy who frequently smoked a forbidden cigarette in the privacy of the pantry. He was beaming with joy now at Mona's return, welcoming her with exclamations of surprise.

"How you've grown, Miss Mona! We're all very pleased to see you home, I'm sure. Her Ladyship is in the drawing room and would you please go straight up?"

Mona ran up the broad staircase. Nothing seemed changed or altered. There was the big picture of the racehorse she had always loved, the snarling head of a tiger that had terrified her as a child, the quaint ivory carvings in a glass case she had always longed to play with. All were in their accustomed places. Only the stairs themselves were narrower than the remembrance, the windows not so lofty.

Their curtains, which had made wonderful hiding-places and been tents of golden cloth concealing Oriental princesses, or the wind-puffed sails of pirate ships, were now but faded brocade, falling in stiff unwieldy folds.

The drawing room door was open, the long room filled with people talking, laughing and eating. Soft lights, artistic hangings and massed flowers made the atmosphere hazy so that it was hard to discover a particular individual. For the moment Mona hesitated on the threshold – then, perceiving her mother, advanced gracefully across the shining parquet floor.

Lady Vivien broke off an animated conversation with an overdressed young-old man. He raised a beribboned monocle with which to observe the intruder.

"Mona, dear child!" Constance Vivien kissed her daughter effusively. "Did you have a good crossing? I hope the car met you. I *loathe* travelling." She raised tragic eyes to her companion. "It is so unnerving. One's nerves are literally unstrung after a day in the train, what with the worry of getting off and packing."

"You, dear lady, should never worry, but make it a privilege for those who delight to wait on you," he responded in a caressing tone.

Rather bewildered, Mona murmured an unheard reply. She had never heard the criticism of a spiteful contemporary of her mother, which, at the time of its remarking, had delighted social London, that "Constance Vivien's conversation was like a Store's catalogue, irrelevant and absurdly inconsistent, passing lightly from subject to subject, leaving her hearer bored and uninterested in them all".

Mona took a cup of lukewarm tea from a side table and sat down unnoticed in a corner.

Old women disguised with paint and soft veils were chattering gaily and skittishly with ornately dressed youths. Old men conversed with languid girls who listened to their tedious conversation with apparent good-humour. Allowing for her age, Lady Vivien was by far the best-looking woman present – tall, with a splendid, if mature figure, straight features and a wonderful complexion, she entirely eclipsed her neighbours.

Twenty-five years before Constance Percival had been the toast of London. Coronets and strawberry leaves had lain in profusion at her feet, but she had scorned them all, flitting from triumph to triumph, conquering old and young impartially. Quite suddenly she had met Bernard Vivien and fallen desperately in love with his looks and fascinating manner. It had been his boast that no woman could resist him and, as Constance was no exception, within a month or so they were married, with plenty of leisure in which to repent their haste.

Lady Vivien had very little affection in her nature. Infatuations for good-looking men were hardly in that category, though becoming more numerous in her middle age than in her callous, triumphant youth. The fierce passion for her husband was long since dead and she had quickly extinguished the lingering flames of his. The only person to whom she was really attached was her son Charles. "He is such a Percival," she would proudly explain, which apparently meant inordinate good looks, combined with an enormous appreciation of his own intelligence and worth. Charles always gave the impression of an almost childlike surprise that he was allowed to walk the pavements with the common crowd. Surely his Creator had originally intended a red-carpeted route for his shapely feet encased by Lobb. In all his twenty-four years, Charles, in Lady Vivien's opinion, had done no wrong. Of course, there had been little escapades – rows at Eton, sent down from Cambridge, an indiscreet chorus-girl affair, "The dear boy was sowing his wild oats," and Charles was really so clever that one day he would surprise everybody.

Constance Vivien had no use for women and even her own daughter was no exception. For five years she had successfully disposed of this unwanted member of the household, but now, unfortunately, the girl had to come out. Luckily, ran her thoughts, Mona wasn't bad-looking although, taking after her father, she lacked the striking appearance of the Percivals and the capacity of remaining permanently in the limelight. But still, someone rich was sure to take a fancy to the child and marry her, and the world would look on Constance as such a successful mother – yet another triumph on her list of accomplishments.

Lady Vivien cast a quick glance round her drawing room. There was no one present at the moment who could be of any particular advantage to Mona. She called her daughter.

"Mona darling, I think you ought to go and rest before dinner. We are going to a dance tonight at – let me see, Moyra Blankney's – quite informal, but I'm having a dinner party for it. Do you know Lady Blankney?" she asked, turning to her neighbour. "Such a dear woman, but a sadly inefficient hostess. So…" Here followed a number of faults and failings interwoven with insincere and gushingly affectionate adjectives.

Mona felt herself dismissed and went upstairs. Annette was unpacking in her bedroom, a charming room with a small *boudoir* opening out of it. Artistically furnished, it held all Mona's childish possessions jealously preserved by Annette. Andrew Lang's *Fairy Tales, The Princess and The Goblins,* the Peter Rabbit books, and a tattered Hans Andersen were all in the bookcase while, sitting in a corner, his beady eyes still protruding, although his coat was somewhat dilapidated, was a Teddy Bear, large, brown and furry. Mona picked him up.

"I suppose I'm too old to play with you now," she said, but she kissed affectionately his hard buttony black nose before she put him down again. Then suddenly she felt the excitement of the new life into which she had plunged sweep over her. There were marvellous enjoyments to be experienced, there were worlds to discover, there was London to explore. She had grown up!

It was so odd. One was a child, living from day to day, eating, playing, sleeping without anxiety or trouble, carefree and careless – and then, almost in a moment, with no perceptible change in one's feelings, the years had gone and one was grown up with responsibility and worries looming ahead.

Still, there was surely compensation in the thought that the capability of emotion could swing as a pendulum in either direction, deep sorrow, great joy, grave seriousness, exhilarating happiness.

The sitting room door opened, disturbing Mona's thoughts, and Charles entered. Faultlessly dressed and well-groomed, smiling his attractive and disarming smile, he was almost as irresistible as his mother believed him.

"Hello, Mona!" He kissed his sister carelessly. "By Jove, you've grown, and into a beauty too. Ma will have to look to her laurels and that won't please the old girl!"

"Charlie, how can you say such things?" remonstrated Mona but laughing in spite of herself.

They exchanged commonplaces with the usual stiffness of relatives who have grown up apart and have no mutual subject of conversation.

"Look here, Mona," said Charles after a slight pause, "are you going to this dance affair tonight?"

Mona nodded.

"Good! Well, listen. Will you do something for me? Give this note to Milly Kingston, Lady Millicent Kingston. Anyone will tell you who she is – tall dark girl, pretty, but a bit of a flyer! If she says anything, let her think I'm in bed with flu. I've said so in the note, and as I swore nothing short of death would keep me from this dance and her charms, pile on the agony."

"But Charles…" expostulated a bewildered Mona.

But Charles was leaving the room.

"A pressing engagement at the Vaudeville Theatre, my dear – stage-door!" he added as he disappeared.

Mystified, Mona gazed at the envelope in her hand, addressed in a dashing handwriting that to a more experienced judge would have told so easily the character of the scribe – the unfinished, careless formation of letters, the sweep of the pen that showed no finesse, no delicacy of perception, and, withal, the slight backward slant.

But before Mona had time to consider Charles's extraordinary behaviour, a footman entered with a message from Sir Bernard asking her to go down to his study if she wasn't too busy. Delighted, she ran downstairs and through the hall where, at the end of a long passage, was her father's private sitting room, a sanctuary from the rest of the house, violation of his peace being an unforgivable sin. Dark leather armchairs, a profusion of books and a large untidy desk dominated the room. It was a thoroughly masculine domain, untouched by femininity.

Her father was alone and standing in front of the fire as she entered. Still unusually good-looking, the cheery *bonhomie* of his face had given way to a fretful expression of anxiety and overwork. He had also taken to brandy in frequent doses to keep his brain clear in the evenings and the reactions were beginning to tell on his nerves and constitution.

He was very fond of his daughter when he remembered her existence and was really glad to see her now. It was the only genuine welcome Mona had received from her family and she hugged him with enthusiasm. They seemed to have lots to tell each other once started, and they sat by the fire chattering gaily, oblivious of time. Strangely alike, yet Sir Bernard was so unmistakably masculine with the virile good looks admired by men as well as women, while Mona with her delicate fragile beauty was almost ethereal.

"And how is the constituency?" she asked him.

"Fairly peaceful," he answered gravely, "but the country is in a disgraceful state, and society will do nothing. They are living on the edge of a volcano. Every ounce of weight added to our defence staves off the threatened culmination, which would bring everyone to their knees and peaceful civilisation falling about their ears. But society refuses to realise the danger. Cocktails and scandal are of greater importance than a national calamity."

Thinking of the women she had seen upstairs and their degenerate companions, Mona understood her father's bitterness. The hopeless position of a prophet who could not make the people listen, a soothsayer whom no one consulted.

Suddenly the clock struck eight and Mona rose with a little cry.

"And dinner is at half-past! I must fly! *Au revoir, mon frère."* She dropped a fairy-like kiss on his forehead and sped away.

"Annette, *Annette,"* she called as she entered her bedroom. "Quick, *quick!* My bath, and I'm going to a dance. Isn't everything lovely!"

As Annette complied, Mona stopped for a moment to look out over the square in the blue twilight. Her face was grave and thoughtful.

'Sally was right! I must make my own life as I want it.'

CHAPTER III

How can one describe the first impression of social life? That butterfly existence, flourishing in the golden sunshine of the world's approval, yet withering in the moment of icy ostracism.

Mona only realised fragments of her first weeks spent in the whirl of gaiety and engagements. Her *début* seemed to unite her to a wheel of hectic sensation – a fairy cinematograph reeled round so quickly as to be unintelligible, untranslatable into words or sane expression.

People hardly mattered – they came and went unnoticed. Youth, unsophisticated, seeks first the material, the pleasures of the inanimate, the eternal Punch and Judy shows that repeat and repeat again in ever-widening circles. Then, when threadbare costumes cease to dazzle, disillusioned, youth turns to the lasting pleasures and sorrows accorded by fellow creatures.

Gradually, tentatively at first, Mona began to find her feet. The little insincerities ceased to wound, the palpable falsehoods ceased to astonish. She was not disgusted or shocked, for, with insight that was born of great sympathy and a faith that found beauty everywhere, she visualised the Pan-like spirit peeping from the dust, creating multi-coloured patterns, erratic but attractive.

Her first dance, her first kiss, little triumphs, tiny sorrows, passed as wind-blown clouds, leaving no mark in a clear sky. Completely unawakened, she was conscious of a force within herself, a power that would have to be dealt with some day, at present dormant, yet oppressing as the stillness of heat before the breaking of a thunderstorm.

London fascinated Mona, even as much as the pantomime of gaieties enthralled. The city with its roar of busy traffic like the engine-room of a vast factory, working unceasingly to create the wherewithal to purchase sweetmeats for the delight of the decorative creatures who inhabited the showrooms of Park Lane, Curzon Street or Berkeley Square, the glass cases where the products of toil are displayed.

Bond Street, with its enticing shops, at which female devotees for ever worshipped. Clothes, clothes, clothes! They fill in a woman's life like cotton-wool, packing her in, enveloping her until they deaden and suffocate every other desire. She forgets to raise her eyes above her neighbour's hat and misses the dancing sunbeams or an iridescent rainbow. She crushes a fragrant violet as she thinks of her new shoes – she misses the joy of motherhood in the preservation of her figure.

Yet a corner of Mayfair is not London. The spirit of her lies in the beauty of the Thames. Misty blue in the morning, and purple with glittering jewels at night. Or her heart throbs as a pale dawn lights the housetops and towers peeping over Admiralty Arch into the broad stretches of the Mall.

In May the fashionable world returned, reopened their houses, and settled down to that three months of doubtful pleasure known as 'The Season'. To them it was but a repetition of a vaudeville show, but to Mona it was a panorama of harlequin delights.

Her fresh beauty, childlike enjoyment and shyly developing wit, made her an instant success, and Lady Vivien was warmly congratulated on her beautiful daughter

– a fact that did not please her insatiable vanity for her own charms.

At a dance given by Lady Dashby in Lancaster Gate, Mona had a tremendous success. Among the tall, somewhat jaded beauties of past seasons, she moved like a dark-eyed nymph or a fairy-tale princess of the Rhine legends. A frock of curious sea-green chiffon made her almost ethereally thin and graceful and her hair was full of strange blue lights. Weary at last, she eluded pursuing partners and stepped on to the long iron balcony that ran the length of the house. One with the shadows, she looked over the park, mystically mysterious with its closed gates, fanlike branches waving as elfin banners over immortal castles, soft purple darkness hiding their glories from human eyesight. She longed to creep through the railings and join the fairy revels in whose existence she almost believed. She smiled at her fancies, then listened to the pipes of Pan, which were surely playing to the water-babies of the Serpentine. What was reality? What was truth? Here, in the shadows, where the road lights curled into the distance like a thousand glow-worms and a warm wind sang strange tunes through the stirring leaves.

A movement beside her made Mona start. She was at the extreme end of the balcony where it joined the next house with merely a space of about two feet between. Leaning over from next door was a young man. It was too dark to see his features distinctly, but he appeared tall and broad, his face and shirt-front showing as white patches against the darkness of his background.

"Undine dreaming behind prison bars," he said softly.

"Stone walls do not a prison make, we are told," Mona replied without thinking. It was a night when the world was too far away even for chaperonage.

"Cold comfort for a chained body even if the spirit is roving free! Are you dreaming of your immortal life on the hills, little prisoner?"

"Rather of the witching pools in the valleys, I'm afraid," answered Mona.

"That is because you are enchanted," he said. "Undine's immortality came in the widening waters from their source in the hills of Olympus! She was chained to the earth by her mortal love," he added. "Are your fetters of such invincible steel?"

"No!" laughed Mona. "Mine are of greedy curiosity of life, of desire to live and to feel the emotions of mankind, to know the depths, so as to appreciate the heights."

"True. Yet even the gods can stoop too low and dare too much."

"And only they can reach the summits," she answered. "To gamble high is at least courageous."

"Would you like to see the sunrise in a fairyland of silver birch trees?" he asked suddenly.

"But how?" Mona questioned.

For answer he pointed over the balcony and she saw standing in front of the house a long silver car, shining like quickened mercury. She looked in silence.

"Sunrise is at four o'clock," he continued. "I will bring you back before the dance is over."

The magic of the night and the soft music from behind them seemed to snap the light bonds of convention. Primitive adventure grew like a golden mirage in a desert of sane conservatism. For a moment Mona hesitated. Then she answered gravely,

"I trust you."

He held out his hands and in a moment had helped her over the tiny chasm between the houses. They stepped through a low window into a darkened drawing room. The only light was over a large picture, making it the only definable object in the room. It was of a French Marquise of the eighteenth century, her hair in a thousand conventionally powdered curls, her patches correctly placed, her laces starched and wired. Yet her eyes were dancing with mischievous enjoyment, her mouth trying ineffectually to be controlled into a tutored Cupid's bow. It was a masterpiece of clever painting, for the laughter portrayed was almost infectious.

As in a dream Mona let her companion lead her down the broad stairs into the hall. The house itself seemed full of unexpected surprises, for a tall brazier of alabaster burned red and glowing, dimly lighting two massive doors of iron and glass. A strangely carved face was illuminated, ivory-white against an ebony background. In front of the fire-place, a huge Irish wolfhound lay watching them, with alert eyes, gleaming in the firelight.

From a cupboard Mona's companion took a fur coat of soft sable and wrapped her in it. Then, opening the front door, they got into the silvered car. From above came the strains of lilting music, excited laughter, and a thousand voices. Beyond lay silence and fairy tales.

The long car moved forward. Through deserted streets, past shuttered houses, empty marketplaces and sleeping watchmen they sped, gradually leaving London lights behind. Putney Common lay disconsolate and empty, its small railing-bound pond unstirred.

A little later they turned sharply to the right down a side-turning towards Wimbledon Common. The narrow lane had hedges that bordered their vision until it passed over a roughly built bridge and widened into rough pasture land, terminating on one side in a small wood. The track led onwards until they rested on the top of a small hill entirely surrounded by trees, tall and slender, their trunks the shining white of the silver birch.

All around was a great silence. The path they had taken was hidden by grey mists, which curled round the tree trunks, like dreams struggling to wakefulness, yet sinking again and again into oblivion. It was the edge of the world to which could come the revelation of forgetfulness.

For a moment Mona sat in silence, then her companion took her hand in his and quoted softly,

"The hour that dreams are brighter and winds colder ... the ebony of night, the red of dawn."

The sky was gradually changing to an iridescent pink, the trees silhouetted, their branches clearly outlined with the fineness of a carving. Crimson, amethyst, amber and sapphire tints shone luminous on the horizon, then crept upwards in scintillating rays. The utter stillness broke as gold, radiant, resplendent, suffused the sky, gleaming and glittering on the silver trees and awakening myriads of tiny bird voices.

With a little sigh Mona turned and beheld her companion for the first time. Dark hair was brushed from a broad brow under which glinted two dark eyes, mocking and laughing intermittently. A firm mouth and jaw steadied the irresponsibility of the rest of the face. Attractively impertinent, he smiled at her scrutiny.

"Thy slave, Undine of the vanquished night."

The embarrassment of the moment passed as Mona laughed.

"Say, rather, my accomplice in crime," she answered.

"And now we must return, prophet and priestess, back from the dawning to the materialism of the common task." He slipped in the gears as he spoke and they drove from the shadows of the trees into the golden clearness of open land. The dawn wind was fresh in their faces, their eyes dazzled yet sparkling in the uplifting youthfulness of day in its infancy.

All too soon London, just stirring, rubbing the sleep from half-closed eyes, enclosed them.

Back past the park to Lancaster Gate where a weary band was still playing extras for a few indefatigable couples. Mona thought it better not to attract notice by entering the front door, so she again wandered through the strange house, noting this time curiously carved furniture and quaint hangings. She stopped for a moment before the picture of the little Marquise hanging in the drawing room.

"She would have enjoyed tonight," she said softly to her companion.

"Adventure was the keynote of her life," he answered. "Desire for it almost a vice in her. She led the youth of the French Court into many a mischievous prank, receiving Royal punishment with complete indifference. She died very courageously in defence of her lover during the Revolution, a jest on her lips, her head held proudly high. But she was very human, Undine. Her veins held rich red blood, not the cold fay-like elixir of immortality."

He held Mona's glance for a palpitating moment. There was a curious little pause of breathless excitement – then with a movement gentle as the smoothness of a nocturne he held her in his arms. For a second he looked at the beautiful face, faintly tremulous, eyes shyly veiled behind dark lashes. Then he bent and kissed the perfect mouth.

Time was indefinable. Then he released Mona and led her towards the window. Without a word he helped her on to her own balcony, retaining her hand across the dividing gulf to kiss its slender fingers.

"*Au revoir,* Undine. The gods have been very kind."

Even as she turned, ready to speak, he was gone. The balcony where he had stood was cold and empty.

With a little sigh she entered the almost deserted ballroom.

CHAPTER IV

The sun shone through the silk curtains, suffusing the room with a kind of golden dimness. Only the tick of the tiny enamel clock on a table by the bed broke the silence – then suddenly, outside the window, a taxi hooted through the square, the sound somehow blunted in the heavy haze of heat rising from the hot tarmac road. With a little sigh Mona turned over and awoke. For some minutes she lay half-dreaming, unconscious of her surroundings. Then she glanced at the little clock and rang the bell. As she waited for her breakfast the events of the night began to return to memory.

And, like most people in the early morning, she was now amazed and astounded at actions that, although impulsive, had seemed natural and inevitable under the gentle influence of Nocturnus.

Romance, criticised with the hideous sanity of breakfast-time, droops its wings and slinks away. How can the eyes see beauty when all the time they regard a plate of eggs and bacon, or the mouth speak poetry when it is full of crackling toast?

With a shudder Mona thought of her mother's comments if she should know of last night's escapade, and quickly came the embarrassing whisper,

"What does *he* think this morning?" And she felt the blood burn in her cheeks. How mad she had been! And yet, it had been a wonderful adventure. The glory of the sunrise and the charm of her cavalier would make even disastrous consequences worthwhile, but she prayed fervently that there would be none. Also, she hoped that a re-meeting with her partner of last night would only occur after time had eliminated her present shamed shyness. But she refused to regret anything – and with a little yawn Mona stretched a white arm out of bed for her engagement calendar.

There were various important entries, fittings for clothes and promised visits to dull relations – then a note for teatime made her frown, starting a serious train of thought.

"Meet Sally and Charles at the Carlton."

"Sally and Charles." Somehow the coupled names worried her. Sally's visits to Belgrave Square were as frequent as Mona's to the palatial residence in Park Lane rented for the Season by Mr. Cutts. Every day they met and discussed the night before, their triumphs, proposals and new acquaintances and, if paternal engagements made luncheon or tea impossible, there were always the mornings in which to walk the Row from twelve to one, or shop diligently, refreshing themselves if exhausted with coffee or ices at Gunter's.

But just lately Mona had noticed that Sally was always eager to call for her, and when she did, Charles was invariably hanging about the hall and instantly suggesting accompanying them to their destinations. One day when the footman announced that Miss Cutts was on the telephone, Mona, on flying to answer it, was surprised to hear Sally say, "Is that you, Charles, darling?" – an instant afterwards making an excuse for her mistake but being noticeably flustered.

'Why should I worry?' Mona asked herself.

Surely nothing could be more desirable than for her best friend to be in love with her brother. Yet somehow she felt antagonistic and unreasonably upset by the whole affair. Sally was such a child, so frank and open in her likes and dislikes which, with the spontaneity of her character, grew quickly into adoration or hatred. There was no light and shade in her affections, no half-measures or semitones.

A passionate temperament and a heart of gold were the compound of Sally's nature. People comprised her world. She was deaf to the call of music, blind to the myriad delights of beauty, yet in her own way extracting greater emotions from life than the sensitive and imaginative. Certainly in youth she would suffer more, because she had no soothing reserves of distraction if the affairs of her heart were contrary and disadvantageous. Her little animal passions would quiver and throb at a hurt, with nothing to calm the waves of self-desires and prevent them from completely overwhelming her, swamping her intelligence, drugging her morals and ideals, blotting out the whitewash of civilisation.

Intrigue, scheming, prevarication were unknown. If Sally wanted something she went straight for it, all the willpower of her own personality and the force of her American blood demanding instant compliance. Trusting, with a childlike innocence, treating crookedness and unfairness as incredible realities, she made every dog a friend until it bit her. And Mona, with the quick insight of the super-sensitive, knew that Charles, the charmer and gallant Romeo to a thousand Juliets, was not the right recipient for Sally's self-entrusted happiness, the first blushes of combined purity and passion, the awakening of the sleeping beauty, the bloom of which can never be replaced once damaged or touched by careless hands.

Charles was too satiated in the contemplation of himself to begin even to realise the value of what he attained so easily – the priceless moment of transition between girlhood and womanhood, the development of feminine emotions, opening slowly like a rose in the warmth of the sun, until gaining the full beauty of perfection, the cold white stillness of purity changing and deepening to the crimson of pulsing love and passion, a combination for which many young men would sell their souls. But to Charles it was but a fresh pair of eyes raised in adoration, a mouth unspoilt by other kisses, a companion only too ready to listen and applaud. For the moment the new fancy held his attention. Yet always in the background hovered other shadows waiting in case *ennui* seized him, watching for the downfall of the favourite.

Marriage from his point of view was a laboured forging of chains which were tiresomely binding, involving enormous trouble to break or elude when their brightness had changed to a dull steel-grey.

Mona puzzled desperately. Yet how could she interfere? Charles would be merely amused by her efforts, treating them as beneath contempt. And Sally, with the impetuosity of the very young and immature, would resent fiercely any interference, however well meant, especially if she were 'in love' with the wholesale infatuation of *le premier fois*, considering "the world well lost..." and spending carelessly the precious coin of friendship in purchasing tempting blossoms that so often would fade and die.

Still worrying, Mona dressed slowly, choosing a soft blue dress and broad-brimmed hat. Then, calling to the companion of all her walks, a small Sealyham, she started for the Park. Togs was only a puppy, very soft and fat, and had been given Mona by her father, a belated birthday present. His one vice was the destruction of leather shoes. He found them absolutely irresistible, and surprised guests in Belgrave Square surveyed with fury the chewed and bedraggled remains of articles that had once been the *objets d'art* of *Messieurs* Pinet or Lobb and had now offered to them by the culprit, with a pleased, contented air as though conferring a favour. They vowed revenge, but the complete innocence of the wrongdoer disarmed them. They laughed, and instantly Togs became the epitome of conceit, frolicking noisily about the room with delight. *"Aren't I clever?"* to be interpreted from his pricked ears, wagging tail, and uplifted voice.

Already, although she had owned him but a short time, he adored Mona. If he were naughty she had but to say, "Oh, Togs!" reproachfully and a small pathetic figure cringed at her feet, apology in his eyes. And when she said, "Walk!" the whole house re-echoed deafeningly to the exuberance of his feelings.

This morning, after the usual excitement, they journeyed fairly peaceably towards the Row. Although it was still quite early the streets were suffocating, the heat of the pavements almost unbearable, and the green trees and their shadows were a paradise after the glare and noise at Hyde Park Corner.

Mona and Togs walked hastily past the overdressed people sitting in hot tight rows, criticising each other in audible whispers, envy, hatred and malice written on most of their over-painted faces.

Further away, almost opposite the Knightsbridge Barracks, the green chairs were unoccupied save for an occasional nursemaid, or a homeless person taking a siesta. Here Mona stopped and rested, while Togs played around, examining each passer-by with interest.

Through the trees shone the Serpentine, and from it came the happy voices of small boys paddling in its coolness, splashing contentedly or watching their more proficient brothers swimming. Far away the hum of busy traffic sounded like the purr of a contented cat, as little disturbing as the buzzing of the bees or small insects circling in tiny clouds in the shadows.

A particularly nice horse coming down the Row caught Mona's eye, for she was devoted to all animals and no mean judge of their good points. This was a dark chestnut with a beautiful head and good action. Mona glanced at the rider, a young man with a seat worthy of his mount. For a moment she thought she knew him, then as quickly realised her mistake. It was merely the first instantaneous impression of familiarity we get with so many people. Yet as she stared, he returned her gaze, and she was sensible of straightforward grey eyes in a sunburnt face, good-looking with the charm of good breeding and healthy living. Then, as their eyes met, Mona turned away her head.

But Togs for some unaccountable reason of his own had taken a savage dislike to the strange horse, and with a little snarl of rage he rushed to its heels barking furiously. The startled animal plunged for a moment, then, as its rider quietened it, let out with both heels at the annoyance behind. With a cry of horror Mona saw Togs lifted into the air, then drop with a thud and lie quite still.

She climbed under the rails and lifted him in her arms and, a moment later, was joined by the young man, who had dismounted hastily. He felt Togs all over, then smiled cheerily at Mona.

"Only stunned, I think. No bones broken, poor little fellow."

Even as he spoke Togs opened his eyes and tried pathetically to wag his tail and lick Mona's hand.

"I'm so sorry it happened." The young man looked really contrite, which, Mona thought, was nice of him, considering that by no stretch of imagination could the occurrence have been his fault.

She smiled back, repudiating his self-accusation.

"Do you think he ought to see a vet?" she asked.

"I honestly think he will be all right, but please will you let me drive you both home? It's the least I can do as an apology, so do let me."

"Thank you," said Mona simply, and they walked, an odd solemn little party, to where his car was waiting under the trees near Albert Gate – Mona carrying a very subdued Togs, he leading the beautiful chestnut mare.

The groom was waiting by the car, a sporting Bentley, and Mona slipped into the front seat.

"Where to?" asked her companion, and, as she told him, exclaimed in surprise, "Why, you must be Lady Vivien's daughter. How extraordinary! I am lunching at your house today. Your mother asked me weeks ago – to meet the American Ambassador."

"How awfully funny!" laughed Mona. "Our introduction has been a little premature."

"And you do forgive me?" he pleaded," because I couldn't sit through luncheon with the knowledge of fury in your eyes and hatred in your heart."

"Of course I do," she replied, "and so does Togs," as the puppy on her lap made feeble attempts to lick his hand.

At the door of Belgrave Square they parted.

"*Au revoir*," he smiled, "we meet anon. I must hurry home to change."

The car rapidly disappeared and Mona turned into the house. As she carried Togs upstairs she remembered that she had forgotten to ask the name of her newly acquired acquaintance.

'I seem to have a capacity for adventures with perfect strangers,' she reflected, 'and extraordinarily charming ones!'

Dark eyes or grey ones? The latter were the most reliable. Then came the remembrance of a farewell kiss, and the colour flooded into her cheeks.

'Yet I'm glad I am to meet the owner of the chestnut again,' she told herself, 'but..." and her question was answered without the need of words.

CHAPTER V

First impressions, especially women's, are generally correct. New acquaintances either rapidly become great friends or drop into that extensive class of persons of whom it can be said, "I've just met them, I think."

Mona, on discovering the name of the unknown rider, discovered also a friend and, more important still, a delightful companion. Peter, Marquis of Leadenhall, was about twenty-seven, tall and good-looking, with a large bank balance and a charming personality. He was greatly sought after by all the match-making mammas and ambitious *débutantes*, but he invariably found them terribly boring, the fact being that he was unusually well-read and intelligent, old for his years, having fought in the War and travelled much further than less fortunate young men. And the chicken feed that his contemporaries called conversation, was as interesting to him as a highly coloured jelly to a hungry man. Innately modest, he always blamed himself for finding women dull and uneducated, thinking himself pedantic and old-fashioned as he yawned at cocktail parties and tried to laugh at jokes that usually seemed inane and somewhat undesirable.

Also, if the truth be known, the modern girl rather embarrassed him. Her frequent use of the word 'bloody' or worse swear words, the freedom with which she discussed sex and all its complexities, the immoderate display of almost nude legs, and the atmosphere of Virginian cigarettes, which drown even the hardiest perfume, left him speechless and tongue-tied. In no ways a prig, for men adored him and at sport his name was a byword, he merely preferred to avoid the society of London's young set, the creators of noise, froth and scandal, but of nothing more tangible or solid.

Mona, with her fresh, unspoilt beauty, high ideals and youthful enthusiasm, was unlike any other girl he had ever known, and when he discovered she could talk intelligently without flirting, enjoy an evening without drinking, and be witty without being vulgar, he quite irrevocably realised he had met the one woman in the world he could love, and worshipped her with all the abandon of a reserved nature with all its depths stirred.

Mona found in Peter a friend worthy of the name, a veritable strong rock of defence if she felt out of her depth or insecure among the whirlpools of her mother's fashionable set. The gushing females who kissed each other effusively and then spat forth venom like poisonous snakes, the half-veiled innuendoes and whispered scandals repeated and re-repeated, becoming more and more exaggerated and fictitious with each fresh repetition, the tight-waisted, young men with their useless lives, their five o'clock appointments and flirtatious efforts, the inanity of their conversations, yet with a sinister note sounding underneath, a thinly veiled throb of unclean passion, incomprehensible to Mona, yet threatening in recurrence. These all made her shudder, then question the cause, and a moment later laugh at herself, as a child in the surety of light forgets the fears of darkness it has left. Yet unconsciously a little maggot was eating its way into her happiness, poisoning her peace of mind, leaving a tiny trail of decay that would presently begin to ache.

Peter realised a little the menace that overshadowed the radiance of Mona's innocence, but he was powerless. The fundamental facts of nature were to her the beautiful blessings of a divine providence, and she was absolutely ignorant of the heinous perversions of man. Vice was a word unknown in her vocabulary. Depraved jokes that the social world considered humorous were beyond her comprehension. He longed to help, to be a guide over the quicksands. Instinctively Mona sensed protection and turned to him with every trouble.

It was a glorious summer, the days blazingly hot, the nights warm and sultry, the dawn bringing the cool winds reviving and refreshing before the sun rose to brilliant and scorching splendour.

Peter and Mona would often journey out of London into the country, starting very early in the morning while the dew still glittered on the grass, a soft blue haze hanging round the trees waiting to be dispelled by the sun which, rising slowly in the pale sky like the gentle prelude to a fierce sonata, shone unnoticed on the curtained and shuttered windows of Mayfair, where the fashionable world was still asleep. Far from the crowded dusty main roads and with only Togs as a chaperon, they explored winding lanes, shadowed by hanging trees, bordered by sweet-smelling hedges covered with dog-roses and honeysuckle. They discovered tiny woods and fields full of moon-daisies, wild orchids, purple and red, and the quaint little yellow flowers that children call "hens and chickens". Here they would eat luncheon provided by Peter in a large basket, from which emerged the most wonderful surprises, chicken, lobster, fresh strawberries packed in cool green leaves, a small packet of chocolate creams or strange American candies, the supply varying every time, but always including a large bone for Togs. When they had eaten, Mona and Peter would lie in the soft grass for hours, half-sleeping, the silence unbroken save for the drone of many bees, the rasp of the crickets and the quick movements of Togs as he snapped at innumerable flies or dug small holes in the ground in the hope of discovering a rabbit.

Later, they would pack up and wander on, talking gaily of many things, revelling more and more in each other's intelligence, the deep knowledge of Peter loving the quickness in Mona to seize a point and dissect it, grasping a subject and on the instant discerning its virtues and failings.

And Mona, appreciating that her own education had just begun, that the school years are but the clearing of the ground where deep strong foundations are to be laid to last for all time, was content to sit at the feet of a Gamaliel whose experience taught the greatest lesson of all – sympathy. Yet it was combined with the Calvinistic creed, which never confused loose morals with broad-mindedness or made allowance for licentiousness on the plea of temperament. Knit together, closer than even a physical embrace could have made them, they were ideal companions in an ideal and golden world. But Peter at times became pupil instead of instructor and realised that book-learning, degrees and the honours of examinations could never lead him to that borderland of reality where fantasies become facts and where dream-forms live.

He had no knowledge and very little imagination about the world invisible. But to Mona fairies were as real as children, ghouls as frightening as burglars. She believed as firmly in the existence of the gods and goddesses of the Hollow Hills as in the Lama of Tibet, knowing more about them than about Henry VIII and his wives. Gravely she told Peter legends and tales of wonderful adventure until the trappings of the world seemed indeed tinsel, and ambition but a cardboard crown.

"Incredible foolishness," said his practical brain. But the sweet, serious face beside him, with the dark truthful eyes and the soft voice that held the genuine note of true belief, was a forceful argument, refuting the cold sanity that we acquire with years and call "grown-up". It revived in Peter the true spirit of childhood, the elixir that had made many a child's heart throb with delicious excitement when he searched Kensington Gardens for Peter Pan, the boy who would never grow up, or, fired by the story of Sir Galahad, took solemn oaths to be "a perfect knight."

Tea was taken at some way side pub, brought to them in a rough arbour in a garden flowering with old-fashioned, sweet-smelling roses. There was fresh bread, homemade jams, fresh-baked scones and milk thick with cream. And then, if they were very happy and Lady Vivien's permission had been obtained, they would linger on for supper and journey back home in the dusky twilight, the hills and trees dark patches against the deepening sky, the first stars gleaming palely, the road silver like a solid stream flowing into the distance as if seeking the sea, determination of its wandering. Gradually the lights of London would glitter like evil eyes and all too soon the rush of busy traffic would break the peace. The squalid streets of the suburbs, alive with humanity, would give way to the order and correct stiffness of the main thoroughfares. Mona would be back at Belgrave Square and the vast house, with its austere silence and unhomely bearing, would be waiting to swallow her up. For Peter there was just an impression of a pale face and slim figure in the gloom of the heavy porch, a soft hand in his and a gentle voice saying so sweetly,

"Oh, Peter, thank you so much."

Then the great door would close with a derisive soundlessness, leaving him with a feeling of irreplaceable loss. He wanted to cry out, to implore Mona to return. But being very English, a moment later he would almost despise himself for being so emotional. In all their expeditions there was no love-making. Like children they played together, only with an intensified power of enjoyment because they felt the contrast to their happy hours in this solidness of social life.

Peter, with the tongue-tied agony of a reserved nature, could not speak to Mona of his love. He wanted to take the very stars from the heavens and lay them at her feet. Yet by the cruelty of nature he could not even tell her that she was beautiful. In bitter irony he heard himself talk to her on every other subject, knew his conversation brilliantly clever, compellingly interesting, found himself more learned than he knew on abstruse topics, until they approached sentimentality, when on an instant he became self-conscious, gauche, monosyllabic, and the golden moment was passed.

Mona guessed perhaps a little of the depths hidden by undemonstrativeness when she heard the story of his life and found it strangely pathetic. It seemed incredible that this much-envied young man, heir to a dukedom, lauded and sought after by the fashionable world, should have a sad history, his childhood and schooldays ruined by lack of affection. But it was only too true. Peter's father, the Duke of Glenac, had married a very beautiful but fragile girl, daughter of a Scottish peer. She had died of pneumonia when Peter was a year old. The Duke had been broken-hearted but, finding solitude insupportable, had married again almost immediately – this time to a vivacious French woman, who bore him one son and then proceeded to shock the world by her *amours* and innumerable scandals. The Duke, an elderly man and never strong, retired more and more into the seclusion of his estate in Scotland, leaving the town house and properties in the hands of his wife. He took little notice of his children. Peter brought back too many painful memories, and the younger boy, Alec, took after his mother and, in the Duke's private opinion, was damnably un-English.

Peter was sent to a private school and afterwards to Eton, but his stepmother never forgave him for being the heir to the dukedom instead of her own son, and to Peter the holidays were weeks of endless correction, when he was made to give up all the toys he most valued to his half-brother, and to bear the punishments for all the misdeeds of both. From the time he was born Alec was caressed, petted and spoilt, but Peter went to bed unkissed, passed the days unpraised, built his baby castles or painted his fairy books with no one to show them to for admiration, no one to give maternal advice. There was nobody to appeal to if things went wrong, or the world became too incomprehensible for baby knowledge. He realised the unfairness in the favouritism shown to Alec, but learnt to set his tiny shoulders, tightly shut his mouth and say nothing. Only sometimes at night when he was all alone in the frightening darkness, because only Alec was allowed a light, did he long for someone to love him. It was impossible to conceive as a definite thought. He just knew he was unhappy and lonely. Burying his face in the pillow so that nurse could not hear, Peter, the little Marquis of Leadenhall, would cry himself to sleep.

The second Duchess of Glenac had been killed in a motor accident at Monte Carlo just before the War in 1914. No one had mourned her particularly. The Duke, now bedridden by creeping paralysis, had hardly set eyes on her for years. Alec, like all spoilt people, had little affection for the hand that showered gifts upon him – he only cared for the gifts. Peter, although emotionally unmoved, was the only person who took any trouble, seeing that her funeral was a befitting one, contriving that her last wishes should be fulfilled. In spite of the memory of his unhappy childhood he felt no animosity, only pity, as he watched the notorious Duchess laid to rest. Her *affaires* and intrigues, sensation upon sensation, hopes and fears, desperate strivings with each newly attracted admirer to look as young and beautiful as her rivals, the misery when with years her triumphs became fewer, her defeats more frequent, heart-tearings, jealousies, uncharitableness, malice… to what end now? A life finished, leaving only one person ready to write an epitaph, and he in 'pity'.

CHAPTER VI

Mona returned to Belgrave Square after a formal luncheon party given at the American Legation. She intended to spend a quiet afternoon and felt her dress of flounced chiffon was ornate and fussy, and the broad-brimmed hat overdressed. She was weary of important functions, of the company of notorieties climbing the steps to fame, of the dreary entertainments arranged "in honour of so-and-so", to "celebrate this and that".

The conversations bored her, and the unhealthy amount of food that was the inevitable accompaniment of each *soirée* was nauseating with rich and sickly creaminess that corresponded with the gushing insincerity of the hosts and the mendacity of the guests.

With an impatient sigh she turned towards the stairs, when a telephone message on the hall table caught her eye.

'Will Mr. Charles Vivien call for Lady Barbie Mills at 2.30 as arranged?'

"Has Mr. Charles had this?" she asked an attendant footman.

"Yes, Miss. Mr. Charles left about a quarter past two in his car."

The news was perturbing, for Lady Barbie Mills was the most notorious *divorcée* in London. Very attractive, with an exotically white face, eyes innocently wide until one looked intently into their dark depths, she was reputedly able to attract any man she desired, holding him hypnotised into a forgetfulness of all else. Ties of honour, business, love or holy matrimony, were pebbles swept before an incoming tide of oblivious passion. If this were true, and she had turned her wandering attentions to the susceptible Charles, it promised badly for Sally's happiness.

Mona had an oppressive presentiment of evil, which materialised into startled fear as she saw Annette waiting anxiously outside her bedroom door.

"Oh, Miss Mona dear, I'm so glad you've come," Annette cried. "Miss Sally is here and very odd and upset. Will you go to her?"

Mona hurried into the darkened room. For a moment she could see nothing and the silence was suffocating with the misgivings of uncertainty. Then she saw Sally, lying on the bed, her muslin dress crumpled, her hair dishevelled, staring fixedly into space. Her face was deathly pale with dark purple rings under the eyes, usually so bright, but the most terrible thing was her expression – lifeless, as though everything, even suffering, had been wiped away. It was the most awe-inspiring portrayal of absolute despair, and Mona stood for a moment in the doorway too stricken even to move towards her friend. Then Sally turned.

"Mona!" Her voice came in a little husky moan as from a great distance and broke the tension.

"Sally, darling!" And Mona was beside her. "What has happened? Tell me ... Don't look like that!"

For a second, silence – then Sally spoke in a curious dull tone, the monotonous note of water dripping on soft stone, devoid of tunefulness.

"Charles is tired of me!"

"Surely not, darling," expostulated Mona, speaking against her own inward conviction, but willing to say anything to take the dreadful drawn look from Sally's face and see again her happy smiles and childlike happiness.

"He told me so last night. He likes Barbie Mills now." Then for a moment the still voice broke. "Oh, Mona, Mona, I love him so!"

"Darling Sally, don't be so unhappy." Mona held her tightly as though to protect this child from the world. She was like an injured animal quivering with pain and not understanding it.

"He was so cruel, cruel!" Sally was trembling now in the agony of remembrance. "He is just bored with me, as he was with all the others. Oh, Mona, why does one always imagine that oneself will be the exception?"

Poor little Sally, voicing in her misery the eternal conceit of human nature – the self-confidence that says, 'This is different!', that thinks itself immune from the snares and pitfalls of its neighbours, only to find in sorrow the house of aspirations is built on sandy ground and is defenceless against wind and storm. Mona felt helpless to comfort Sally. There is so little one can do for mental wounds – they ache and smart with all the agony of physical hurt, yet the onlooker is powerless to dress or bandage them.

At intervals, Sally went on speaking, vaguely, as though to herself, reviewing the past.

"We were so happy – that day at Ranelagh he loved my yellow dress – the garden at night he said my eyes shone in the darkness. We were to have had such a wonderful summer, my first season ... Ascot, Lord's and then Cowes ... the still nights, the water lapping round the yacht, and Charles. Oh, Mona, Mona, what shall I do? How can I bear the loneliness?"

"Don't, Sally!" Mona's eyes were wet. The fearsome shattering of plans that youth makes so far ahead, mapping out a lifetime in a few minutes, anticipating no obstacles, only a broad, easy road, without stones and pitfalls – Castles in Spain, doomed to destruction. She protested with a little cry, holding Sally closer.

"Darling, there are lots of other men in the world. Don't break your heart over one worthless one. You will forget one day, meet a really nice man and marry him."

For a moment after Mona's outburst there was silence then in a strange, eerily quiet way, Sally answered,

"No nice man will want to marry me now."

"Sally!" Mona paused for words. "You don't mean. Oh, Sally, you can't!"

"Yes." Sally's answer was weary beyond words. "What does it matter now?"

"But aren't you frightened, Sally, is it all right?" Mona stammered.

"Oh, quite!" A terrible smile, cynical and bitter, curled the corners of her mouth. Then the dreadful calm broke and Sally, shaken with sobs, clung to Mona and the welcome tears were a relief.

"Mona, I loved him so. He was so persuasive and I was frightened of losing him – and now I've lost everything. Oh, God..." and Sally sat up suddenly, her face transfixed with an agonising fury. "I hate him, *I hate him.*" Then, as the second passed, she made a limp gesture of helplessness. "But I don't – I love him."

All the afternoon Mona sat with her, soothing and quietening, bathing the hot head and eyes with *eau-de-cologne*. At last, worn out physically and mentally, Sally fell into a deep sleep, and Mona rose to leave her. She looked down at the pathetic little figure, the face tear-stained and blotched like an unhappy child's, yet, in the elasticity of youth, with the colour already creeping back into the pale cheeks and lips. There was the quick intake of the breath as in a child after crying.

Suddenly Mona felt very old. She went into her sitting room and looked out of the window over the trees. She wasn't shocked by Sally's confession. She felt as though she were looking at it from the experience of generations, with a great world-wise knowledge of human nature. In that moment she saw only the pity of youth spilt like wine in the begriming dust, soiling its purity, besmirching white garments with the stains of uncleanness. Morality, religion, convention seemed somehow unimportant. It was the hurt to the immortality of personality, the cramping of the godlike essence that, running through our veins, lifts us high above the animal, strengthening with our efforts to rise and becoming weaker as we fall.

And Charles! At the thought of him the verse came to her mind, "And whosoever shall offend one of these little ones, it is better for him that a millstone were hanged about his neck, and he were cast into the sea."

Sally, the innocent, trusting child! It was not the physical injury that counted, it was the deliberate massacre of her ideals, the smashing of fairy-tale castles, the trampling of golden dreams. With the splendidness of youth her wounds would heal, the misery pass. But the scars would always remain, and the delicate fabric of perfect happiness, once touched by careless hands, loses the bloom of its lustre. Only once in a lifetime do the flowers in our secret garden of fantasies bloom to perfection, fanned by the winds of innocence. To the very few, the very favoured, perhaps only to one person in our lives, do we open the gates with the key of love. Too often do we find too late they are merely trespassers, ruthlessly picking the flowers, to leave them dying by the roadside, scoffing at the ambitious little buildings we have erected, destroying our temples with laughter. Then, when we are barren, they leave us to a desert of desolation.

Then the clearness of her vision passed and Mona became but a human girl, seeing for the first time primeval passion unveiled and hating it with the full force of a fastidious temperament.

Suddenly she looked Nature in the face and found it an animal, stalking its prey to devour, waiting for a loophole in the stockade of intellectual defence, confident of victory with the intuition of a seasoned hunter. For the moment, blinded by inexperience, she could not comprehend the intricate workings of the divine among all the threads of life, lining the dusky colours, so that only after searching could the truth be revealed, the casual and indifferent observer receiving but a surface impression of darkness, human nature being belittled and distorted as though seen through the wrong end of a telescope.

Her emotions seemed to be beating chaotically, like waves in a storm. Mona wanted to hide herself from the relentless fingers of a life that dragged its victims into the whirl of sensations, making them feel to the utmost of their capability. It was impossible for her to conceive that in the future she would crave the abduction, long to be in the centre of the surging maelstrom, piteously repudiating the calmness and security outside the theatre of vitality.

Now she prayed for deliverance from the remorseless tide that was sweeping her into strange currents. Her quiet haven was threatened, the waters tempestuously stirred. Almost imperceptibly, yet intuitively, she sensed the rising storm. Panic-stricken, she wanted to fly, yet there appeared no way of escape. With the courage of a man clutching a straw, she hoped her fears were groundless, the excited tremors of an overstrained brain.

CHAPTER VII

That night Mona was taken to a dance given by Lady Stanhope in Park Lane. She had pleaded to be allowed to stay at home, but Lady Vivien had proved obdurate, demanding a real excuse and, when Mona could not give one, insisting on her company.

Miserable at leaving Sally, Mona dressed carelessly, dreading the evening before her and her mother's party of frivolous people. She was a striking figure when she entered the ballroom, her face pale and unhappy, her skin noticeably white against the severe black of her dress, which, falling in graceful folds, made her slightness more pronounced than usual. Beside the gaudy glittering *toilettes* of her party, she looked like a beautiful etching hung amidst badly executed oil-paintings. The delicate finesse of her immature figure showed up the crude lines and coarse contours of her companions.

Given in one of London's largest ballrooms, the decorations alone costing enough to feed a hundred starving families for a year and the bandmaster commanding a larger salary than the Prime Minister, the ball was one of the most successful functions of the season. But afterwards Mona could remember nothing of its brilliance. She danced as one in a dream, hating the stupidity of her partners, and the crowd around her. Her brain worked without conscious thought, for apparently her conversation if not original was in no way peculiar. At one moment she listened to herself as to a stranger describing a game of polo witnessed at Ranelagh the afternoon before.

At last she slipped away into the tiny garden, decorated with coloured lights, but almost deserted while the music played, save for one or two couples half-hidden in the shadows and engrossed in themselves. She found an empty and obscure corner, made by an alcove in the outside wall of the house, and sat down, hoping the search of her eluded partners would be unavailing.

Thoughts formed in her mind, then passed, as swallows in their flight, too swiftly for coherence, when suddenly she heard voices quite close to her. A couple were sitting on the sill of the open window, and while she hesitated about moving, revealing her presence, abandoning her hiding-place, or remaining an unwilling eavesdropper, she recognised the caressing tones of the man. It was Charles! She hurriedly decided to move, yet as she summoned up courage, Charles in a deep insistent voice said,

"God, Barbie, you're marvellous tonight. You drive me mad!"

The woman's soft laugh was intoxicated with passion.

"Homicidal lunacy?" she questioned.

"I don't want to kill you ... yet." The answer was almost a whisper and the voice faded away on the last word. In the pregnant pause that followed Mona knew they were kissing each other. Kissing while Sally, discarded, forgotten, sat at home in misery.

With an almost audible cry of horror Mona rose and passed the still embracing couple, the passion of their enfolding arms nauseating her, but making them oblivious of her presence. She fled down the garden as from a pursuing evil, then paused on the threshold of the ballroom. Blinded for a second by the brilliant glare of the lights, seeking a familiar face, suddenly she saw Peter! Dear Peter*!*

Steadily making his way through the crowd towards her. His kind face anxiously questioned the unhappiness in hers. With a sigh of relief she seized his arm.

"Peter, I am so glad you are here. I want to go home – now – at once." The insistence in her voice surprised him, but he answered quite calmly.

"Of course. My car is outside."

Mona got her cloak and, when she came down, found Peter waiting with the car, having sent away the chauffeur. She got in beside him and he drove quickly with her into the coolness of the park, for it was still early and the gates were open. He knew so well the power of beauty to soothe Mona if she was upset, and he drew up under the trees near the Serpentine, which was unstirred as the surface of a mirror and reflected the overhanging trees and shrubs in the light of the moon. It was very quiet. After the noise of the jazz band, the chatter of the crowded ballroom with its close atmosphere and tiring brilliance, the silence relieved the tension like a breath of sea air on a heated brow.

After a moment Peter took Mona's hand in his and the next instant she was in his arms, sobbing with the abandon of a child who has been hurt. He held her without speaking until the storm somewhat abated, realising that it was the pent-up emotion of many hours. As she grew calmer he murmured little words of comfort, producing a clean silk handkerchief to replace a wisp of lace which was useless for anything but decorative purposes.

At last Mona moved and lay back against his shoulder, half-exhausted, the tears still shining on her wet lashes, very black against the pallor of her face.

"Thank you, Peter." Her voice was a broken whisper.

Then Peter found words, and they came like the slow but sure bursting of a dam unable to resist the pressure, but strong enough to let the waters through only gradually.

"Mona darling, let me take you away from all this. I don't know what has upset you, but I know you hate this life and all it entails. We will travel, dear, and live in the country and do anything you like – only trust me and let me look after you. I swear you shall have anything you want in the world. Won't you marry me, Mona?"

There was silence for a long moment. Swiftly through Mona's thoughts ran pictures of Peter, Peter in the country, in London, alone with her, or with other people. Always kind and considerate, always interesting. Reliable – he would never let one down. A promise was a before-God oath to Peter, his word an unbreakable bond whatever the cost. Unselfish in everything because he considered himself too unimportant to worry about, the comfort of his companions his first thought.

If Peter loved her, she ought to be the happiest woman in the world, because he would be so utterly selfless in his devotion, ready to give her anything she desired. And she would be safe with him, safe from this incomprehensible whirl around her. He was an escape.

Mona turned towards him, again clinging to him desperately.

"Yes, Peter dear. Take me away, right away from everything."

"Darling!" Peter's heart was full. He had obtained his objective. He could have sung a *Te Deum*, written a poem of happiness, composed an oratorio of thanksgiving, but his lips were sealed. He buried his face in the soft masses of Mona's hair, a look of utter contentment on his face. They sat thus for several minutes, then in a strangled voice, Mona said,

"Peter, I can't face it – the fuss and the excitement – especially from Mother, all the smirking beastliness. Why are you so important?"

Peter considered, then answered gravely.

"Why should we tell anyone, dear? Let's just get married and tell them all afterwards. By the time they have started to congratulate us we shall be far away."

"Oh, Peter, *could we?*" There was a thrill of excitement in the young voice – the romance of an elopement is a sensation that never ceases to enthral the youth of every century.

"Why not? I have no family to be hurt or offended. My father is too ill and, anyway, would be uninterested. The only person to be considered is your mother."

"Oh, Peter, must we consider her? She would only enjoy it because you are a marquis. If I were marrying anyone else she would clothe me and celebrate the occasion because it would be the right thing to do. But really she would have no feelings in the matter. She will not miss me as a daughter, because she has never wanted me. Daddy will be only too glad to avoid a ceremony that would require his attendance, and Charles...

Her voice sharpened on the word and Peter, sensing a tragedy, probed the question no further.

"Then it is settled, darling. Now..." but the triumph in his voice altered unmistakably, the end of his sentence died away.

Startled, Mona moved in his arms, raising her head in a vain attempt to see his face.

"Why? Oh, what's the matter?" It was the frightened cry of an almost rescued alpine climber, who feels the rope cracking even as he reaches the top of the chasm where destruction has been baulked of her prey.

"You are under twenty-one. I can't obtain a licence without your parents' consent."

There was a tragic silence between them after Peter's explanation. And Mona, with morbidly vivid imagination, saw pictures of the future that filled her with despair. Endless entertainments at which Peter and she would be shown off like *mannequins* at a dress parade. Peter would display the glamour of his position while she would be regarded with all the strange, unexplainable curiosity with which society encircles an engaged girl who is making a good match. The forced confidences her girlfriends would insist on, thinking themselves defrauded if they were not regaled with detailed accounts of "when he first kissed her", "What he said", "If she expected to enjoy her honeymoon". Question upon question, each more impertinent than the last. The married women who would offer her advice, the nervous excitement before the wedding, even the look in the maid's eyes who would call her on the auspicious morning. They would strip her naked and gloat over her unviolated virginity. She could not bear it.

"Peter, what can we do?" She appealed to him for protection – the cry that mankind can never listen to unmoved.

"Could we tell your father?" Peter spoke slowly, as though the idea materialised with his words.

"How clever you are! Daddy wouldn't tell a soul, he would understand!" The rescue could be effected after all – the rope would hold.

"We will ask him tomorrow, darling." Peter was gloriously happy again. "And I think the formalities will only take a day or two – will that be all right for you?"

Such ordinary words, but he waited for his answer as a prisoner in the dock awaits the judge's decision – breathlessly.

"Yes, Peter." It was the answer of one who in relief lays the burden of trouble and worry oppressing them on the shoulders of another. Secure in the firm arms Mona felt immune from the world. Her last doubts vanished and she raised her head from his shoulder. Through the darkness she met his eyes looking down into hers, dear, reliable Peter, unchanged, unaltered, always her friend.

"You will be very kind to me, won't you, Peter?" she said with a little sob, hardly knowing the reason for her question, unless an almost unconscious premonition warned her how much his promise was to matter in the future.

"Always, darling," he answered gravely, her meaning incomprehensible to him also. For how could he be anything else to this wonderful being who was to be his especial care? If he realised in his overwhelming happiness that Mona only loved him as a friend, he considered it a perfectly natural occurrence. For her to have been otherwise would have been an inconceivable miracle. He was content to worship his deity from afar, only too willing to pour the fruits of the earth at her feet if that would bring a smile to her lips. He had yet to learn that feminine deities demand the moon and the stars as well as the earth yet perversely adoring the wooer who withholds both, just out of reach. Solemnly they sat in silence, gazing into the darkness, both a little awed by the step they had taken, Peter already shouldering his new responsibilities with intentions that had almost the nature of oaths so serious were their purport. And Mona – her thoughts were for herself. She was entering a haven of peace, the waters smooth with the oil of friendship. It was all she desired, all she wanted from life – a safe anchorage. With the impetuosity of youth she planned the years ahead, seeing a life of quiet contentment, without storms, without squalls. She did not understand in her innocence that all characters must be tried by fire – tried like steel – and that the truest happiness is not to be found by inertia. Youth must battle ceaselessly to attain comforts for old age.

On the doorstep of the house in Belgrave Square Peter bade Mona good night.

"Good night, dear Peter," she answered, and held up her lovely face like a child.

He kissed her very gravely, then turned away.

She waited a second as though disappointed, an unconscious expectation of something more. Then she entered the house.

"Sally was right. I shall marry my Duke," she thought. Then she gave a little sigh. Somehow there was something missing. She felt curiously unelated.

CHAPTER VIII

Mona, Marchioness of Leadenhall, leant against the fence that divided the paddock from the drive and watched her husband breaking into a saddle, a newly purchased pony. Peter, in a loose riding shirt and perfectly fitting breeches and boots, was very pleasant to look upon. A look of determination vied with one of exhilaration in his fight with the capering, bucking animal beneath him. Mona felt she had never noticed before the wiry strength of his muscles and the poise of his head on the straight square shoulders. Ruffled hair gave him a boyish look, almost recklessly handsome, unlike the impression one usually received.

They had been married three weeks and two days ago had returned from their honeymoon to Peter's house in Somerset. Left to him by a great-uncle, it was a perfect old thirteenth-century building of grey stone, standing on a hill and looking towards the end of the Cheddar Range. Wonderful woods stretched as far as the eye could see and sloped down the valley through which ran a river journeying to the mouth of the Bristol Channel about five miles away. Taylsea Court was renowned for its splendid preservation and historic interests. Mona loved the diamond-paned windows and panelled rooms, the ancient stone courtyard and secret passages. Outside long terraces bordered velvety green lawns, and beyond the garden were orchards of cherry, plum and apple trees. In an Elizabethan walled-in garden of paving stones and small box-hedges grew old-fashioned roses and night-scented stock, together with lavender and mignonette. Behind the house dark fir and pine trees made a perfect background.

The peaceful beauty around, the wonderful restful atmosphere of the old house, and the calm of her new life were to Mona supreme happiness. Peter and she had been married at St. Paul's, Knightsbridge, at nine o'clock, after an engagement of two days. It had been a wonderful morning with a promise of great heat. Mona, in a dress of the palest blue chiffon, a simple hat to match, carried a few perfect pink roses in her hands. The chauffeur and the verger were the only witnesses, For Sir Bernard, although giving his consent wholeheartedly, was too frightened of losing his peace and quiet to risk Lady Vivien's wrath if he attended a ceremony from which she had been barred. He even hoped, secretly, that in her ignorance of the formalities of a special licence, she would be unaware of his participation in the conspiracy. So without the presence of kith or kin, Peter and Mona started a new life, the union performed by a disinterested curate. Yet the silence in the beautiful church, the sun throwing a thousand coloured rays through the stained-glass windows on to the white altar and its gilt reredos, lighting the pale face of the bride, was a blessing from Heaven itself. The sun deepened in golden glory until it utterly eclipsed everything in its brilliance. Mona and Peter seemed to stand alone, bathed in an immortal light – radiant, divine.

"Those whom God hath joined together, let no man put asunder," rang in Mona's ears as, for the last time, she signed her maiden name. For one moment came the quick doubt, 'What have I done?'

It made her turn and look at Peter. But the sight of his dear face, alight with happiness, his steady eyes seeking hers, was reassuring. On an impulse she took his arm.

"Oh, Peter, are you glad?"

"Beyond words, my darling," he answered, and to a wedding-march of their own they had walked together down the aisle.

Outside solemnity fled and Togs, waiting patiently in the car for their return, was shown the new wedding-ring, and he congratulated them in his own noisy inimitable way. The next two hours were rather frightening, but on the whole the family took the news well. And, with Peter beside her, Mona felt she could face all the devouring lions in London.

Lady Vivien was torn between pleasure at the social importance of her son-in-law and anger at being deprived of a function at which she could have held the centre of the stage and enjoyed the envy of her friends. But the deed was done – it was too late now. So she smiled and called them "naughty children", whispering, as she kissed Mona, "You have played your cards well, my dear. I'm delighted."

"But I didn't..." Mona started to say, then stopped herself. That Peter's title was a disadvantage would be to Lady Vivien an inconceivable aspect of the marriage.

At last it was all over and they started off in Peter's large touring car. The only person Mona minded leaving was Sally, a pale, sad Sally, whose look of misery vanished for one moment when she heard the news only to return as she said goodbye.

"I shall miss you terribly," she whispered. "You will write?"

And Mona promised. Then, stepping into the car, she drove away with her husband, feeling curiously unstrange because it was Peter.

*

Honeymoons are nerve-racking and emotion-straining at the best of times, and if you are already weary of everything save peace, they merely become irritating and unnecessary. Mona and Peter soon longed for the quiet of the country. So, after a few days at Deauville, a night or two in Paris, and a short journey south, they returned to Taylsea Court.

Mona never forgot her first view of the house. They motored down from London, where they had picked up various necessities for the country, including the beloved Togs and new clothes for Mona. The journey had taken most of the day, and as twilight fell Mona was half asleep in the front of the car beside Peter, who was driving. Suddenly he stopped the car on a bridge which spanned a small river. "I want you to see Taylsea from here," he said.

Mona looked up. They were down in a valley, and high above them, on either side, towered dark woods. A blue mist was rising around them, creeping up towards the trees, a pale sky held one star, glimmering like a perfect jewel. Silhouetted against the purple background, its gables sharply defined, the lights in the windows burning like welcoming beacons, stood Taylsea Court. To the imagination it seemed a fairy house from some illustration of the Rhine Legends. Through the darkness the drive leading up to it gleamed like a golden pathway – surely the road to the heart of happiness.

Peter was inarticulate, but he saw the beauty and loved it as much as Mona. He wanted to tell her so, to say,

"This is our home, darling, yours and mine, and our happiness shall be as beautiful. You and this are all I ask in the world because I love you both beyond words, beyond expression." But such speech was impossible to Peter, so he merely said,

"Well, darling?" and awaited Mona's reply.

"It's too, too lovely. I didn't know anything could be so wonderful and yet so real. Don't you love it, Peter?"

"Yes," said Peter noncommittally, and drove on.

*

Mona's bedroom looked out over the valley and that night she had stood by the open window and gazed at the solemnity of the hills. They seemed so strong, unchangeable, watching through the silence of the night for the break of day, listening for the music of the cool winds blowing up from the sea and playing strange tunes through the ancient trees that had braved the violence of many fierce storms. Strange stories the wind whispered, tales of adventure, of stolen ships, of broken lives, of faithful hearts, secrets that the forest pondered in silence while the hills laughed. They had remained while generation after generation of men had passed by the drama of a century merely a swiftly acted pageant. Tragedy or comedy – what matter? Tomorrow it is finished. This house, the stage of perhaps a thousand dramas, the womb that had conceived a thousand offspring.

And Mona, its new chatelaine, prayed to the hills, the guardians of her home, that her life should be one of happiness and contentment, secure under the protection of their inviolability.

Peter was quietening the frightened pony and at last managed to make him trot gently round and round the field. Then he stopped near Mona and dismounted.

"That's enough for today, I think," he said, as Mona patted the tossing head and pulsing neck.

They walked together up to the stables, Togs at their heels, the pony too tired to protest any more.

As they returned towards the house the butler met them with a telegram. Peter opened it.

"From Alec," he told Mona. "He is motoring past on his way to London and wants a bed for the night."

Mona gave the necessary orders and the servant departed.

"I am very anxious to see your half-brother, Peter. Is he like you?"

"Not really. All the Gordons have a kind of family likeness, but Alec resembles his mother. He has that polished manner which is so French, and he is far more amusing than I am, darling."

"I don't want you to be amusing," said Mona affectionately. "I like you just as you are, my dear old Peter."

They were standing on the lawn under a large, spreading tree. The bees were humming among the flowers that scented the whole garden with their wonderful fragrance. Mona in a pale green dress, without a hat, her dark hair just stirred by the breeze, suddenly seemed to Peter very young, a mere child who ought to be dancing carelessly on the surface of realities, basking in the sunlight of a butterfly existence. Insistently he turned her round to face him.

"Mona, do you think you will ever get bored with me and this quiet life? Will you regret the fun you have left behind? You are so young, dear, to settle down."

A little cloud passed over the bright eyes looking into his.

"One day, Peter, perhaps I will be able to tell you why I was so unhappy the night we..." she smiled up at him, "...we got engaged. But it isn't my secret. I can only say that I was terribly upset and miserable. There seemed nothing tangible in life save unspeakable horrors. And then you came, Peter dear, and took me right away to this..." She made a little gesture at the beauty around them, then added simply, "I am so happy."

Unspeakably content, Peter bent his head and kissed his wife. For the moment Mona clung to him. But it was the protection of his arms she craved, not the touch of the arms themselves because they were his.

The sound of a car rapidly approaching disturbed them and a moment later they perceived it climbing the long drive.

"I expect it is Alec, darling," said Peter. "I will go and meet him."

"We will have tea out here," Mona replied, "so I will wait for you both."

Peter hurried away and Mona sank into a wicker chair covered with soft cushions and lazily watched the servants bring out an appetising tea on large trays. Peter, like all men, hated a finicking little meal of thin bread-and-butter, tiny sickly cream cakes and a magnificent spread of silver and priceless china. He liked an old-fashioned schoolroom tea, a new loaf to cut himself, a huge pat of fresh butter, home-made strawberry jam and a fruit cake so full of currants and raisins as to be reminiscent of plum pudding. Mona laughed at his greed yet found that the country air and exercise made her appetite a good second to Peter's, while Togs threatened to become a gourmet of the worst type.

'I must remember to buy some new tea cloths,' Mona thought and laughed a little. How domesticated she was getting! As a matter of fact she enjoyed housekeeping, confessing her ignorance and willing to learn from Mrs.

Mullins, the old housekeeper, who had been at Taylsea Court for over forty years. She had reigned supreme because it had been a bachelor household, and she had been nervous of a new feminine influence, sensing a violation of her rights. She had looked very uncompromising during her first interview with Mona. Her black silk dress was fastened with a huge cameo brooch, her grey hair brushed into a tight knot, the stern rigidness of her features making her look like a character from Dickens. A hard woman, with no sentimentality in her nature, when she had first entered the room Mona, with a disarming smile, had held out her hand.

"How do you do, Mrs. Mullins?" she had said. "I am enchanted with Taylsea Court. I'm afraid I am very ignorant to be the mistress of a large house. But I am relying on you to teach me. In the meantime, I want things to continue as they always have, because I'm sure your arrangements are far more sensible than any I could suggest."

Mrs. Mullins had been victimised immediately. Mona's charms were inevitable. The old housekeeper was not to be pushed on one side as though forty years' devoted service counted for nothing. Beaming with good-nature, she showed her treasures proudly, the rows of home-made jams and pickles in the stillroom, the fine linen sheets and embroidered pillow-cases, the kitchenware shining like polished silver, and lastly, most precious of all, her book of recipes, collected from countryfolk and many friends long since dead, recipes for preserving fruits, for baking, for distilling strange medicines and balms. It was the greatest favour she could confer, and Mona, who realised this, thanked the old woman accordingly.

"How clever of you, darling!" Peter had said when she told him about it. "Mullie has a heart of gold, but only one person in a hundred discovers it under the gruff exterior."

Tea was waiting, yet the two men delayed and Mona was growing impatient when they appeared at last at the end of the terrace. She watched them walk towards her.

Lord Alec Gordon was just a little taller than Peter and thinner in a subtle way, wiry with a grace that generally made him look overdressed – and now a perfectly fitting flannel suit against Peter's rough riding clothes made Mona think of his French blood. He gave the impression, even at a distance, of polish.

She rose as they joined her, and as Peter introduced them Alec swept off his hat with an extravagant gesture. For a moment they both stared at each other, recognition striving with memory in their eyes. Then Alec spoke gaily in a well-remembered mocking voice.

"Hello, Undine! Still dreaming?"

CHAPTER IX

Mona told Peter of her first meeting with Alec. Although quite innocent, it was a difficult story to tell. Words could not describe the impulse which had drawn her into almost a flirtation with a perfect stranger. Feeling rather guilty, she omitted the *finis* of the evening, the kiss under the picture of his ancestress. It would somehow make the situation too embarrassing to be pleasant – an *affaire* with her husband's brother.

As for Alec, he never left the subject alone.

"You have broken my heart, Peter," he said again and again. "I meet the most wonderful girl in the world, become so dazed and up in the skies that I forget to ask her name, and after endless searching find my brother has married her behind my back. What's more, I'm not even asked to the wedding!"

"But there wasn't one! I mean…" said Mona laughing and correcting herself at Alec's look of assumed horror, "there was no dressed-up society function, no bridesmaids and orange-blossom."

"Of course not," answered Alec. "Elfin princesses don't get married like that. The bridegroom goes out into the woods at dawn and stands in the middle of a mushroom-ring. He shuts his eyes, wishes, and turns round three times. When he opens them, he finds a lovely princess beside him, clothed in mist, her jewels of glittering dewdrops. Lucky Peter!"

But Peter felt out of his depth during this sort of conversation and would wander away to look at his horses, leaving Alec and Mona to talk on, of fairies, gnomes and nymphs. Yet the legends always seemed to veer round to personalities. However hard she tried, Mona always found herself in the midst of a half-flirtation. She put it down to Alec's French origin. Yet it annoyed her when a chance remark, though uttered too indefinitely to be challenged, brought the colour to her cheeks.

His resemblance to Peter was noticeable in the small habits and individual movements which close relations copy from one another or acquire in the blood of their forebears. Mona remembered the familiarity of Peter's bearing when she first saw him. But the impression had not been strong enough for her to connect it with her companion of the night before. Perhaps it was the contrast in their characters that made their facial distinction greater than the mere variation of features. Alec did not exactly 'wear his heart on his sleeve', but his emotions were near enough to the surface to give an impression of uncontrol. In point of fact, the lack of reserve was wilful. Alec's one hobby was experimenting in sensations. Unluckily he did not confine this pastime to himself, and his past was strewn with discarded 'copy', which, not unnaturally, earned for him a just if unpleasant reputation. However, he had many good qualities, and in contradiction to all popular sentimental belief, he was adored by children and animals. Also, to refute poetic justice or its equivalent in the minds of amateur Sherlock Holmeses whose bible is *The Rosary* and whose religion the creed of Ethel M. Dell, on acquaintance Alec was as charming to plain women of a certain age as to their more fortunate sisters. The twists of human character afford an endless study. There is no regulation mould, there are no stereotyped lines of development. It is as easy to predict the future of an acquaintance as to find a contentedly married couple.

Alec's visit, intended for one night, extended to over a week. He made himself thoroughly at home, altering everybody's plans to suit himself with an incorrigible charm that frustrated all dispute. The weather was glorious and they were all intensely energetic. Mona would ask a neighbour in to make up a four at tennis, and they would play set after set until the women owned themselves exhausted. Then, rushing to Alec's racing car, they would cover the five miles to the sea in almost the same number of minutes. Undressing under the cover of friendly rocks – somewhat hard to find on the flat marshlands that border that part of the Channel – they would plunge into the cool waves, a sensation too delicious for description. As Alec put it, "One can almost hear the sizzle of cooling heat as one enters the water."

Peter never forgot the first time he saw Mona in a swimming costume, the dark green silk tight to her figure, the small head poised on the straight shoulders, she was like a slim boy, unquestionably feminine, intoxicatingly elusive, like a waking dream. Her white arms and legs, beautifully shaped, her quick movements and lilting laughter made the illusion all the stronger. He felt that at any moment she might sink into the waves and disappear to a palace beneath the sea, lost for ever to human eyes.

"Undine!" A perfect name for her black-and-white slenderness, and the blue and green that were so essentially the colours belonging to her. A name given her by Alec. Peter would have given worlds to have thought of it himself. He wanted to run to Mona and seize her in his arms, carrying her away from all these people to where they could be alone. He wanted to tell her she was his, belonging to him. He wanted to whisper how beautiful she was like that, to pour out some of the poetry in his soul at her feet, to tell just a little of what he felt so acutely. An impossible ambition!

Yet Alec – Alec the debonair – was saying in his half-serious, half-mocking voice the things Peter craved to articulate. Holding Mona's tiny hand in his as he helped her over the rough shingle, complimenting, flattering and teasing, until her laughter rang out again and again. Then, with a sudden movement, she eluded his grasping fingers and ran lightly to Peter who, standing alone, feeling like a darkening cloud in the perfection of a clear sky, was hating his unsociableness, yet unable to cast away the depression creeping over him.

"Peter, darling," a soft arm crept through his. Mona had sensed his lonely-little-boy-at-a-party feeling, "will you carry me into deep water?"

A perfectly happy Peter lifted his wife in his arms. The day was suddenly overwhelmingly glorious again. For a few moments he held her, then with a little laugh she slipped into the water and swam out to sea.

*

"I must really leave tomorrow," said Alec from the depths of a comfortable armchair, a trail of blue cigar smoke rising above him like incense trying ineffectually to reach the heavens.

"You have said that every day for the last week," answered his hostess, pausing from the contemplation of a mass of flowers in a basket beside her. "Alec, do you think pink roses or blue delphiniums in this Chinese vase?"

"Roses," said Alec absently. "I mean it this time. Tomorrow I must be in London, 'though Hell should bar the way', as the highwayman said, according to Mr. Alfred Noyes. Will you miss me, Undine?"

"Of course I shall," said Mona heartily. "Peter and I want you to come again very soon."

"Don't say it like that," said Alec disconsolately, "in that idiotic bread-and-butter voice with that inane 'I-am-the-good-hostess' look on your face."

"How irritable you are today, Alec!" Mona put down her flowers and regarded him with an Amused smile. "I'm very sorry you are going away, but you don't expect me to weep public tears on your shoulder, do you?"

Quite suddenly Alec got up from his chair and threw away his cigar. He walked over to where Mona was standing and put a hand on her shoulder, his sleek head bent towards her, his dark eyes strange and curiously unfathomable in their expression.

Mona felt her heart give an unexpected thump. An odd wave of excitement seemed to be creeping up her throat. It was a sensation totally unlike anything she had ever experienced before, and for a moment she quivered in his hold. A little smile flickered across his face.

"One day I'll make you pay for that last remark, Mona darling," he said, the last word quite deliberately, dragging out the syllables. Then, removing his hands from her shoulders, he walked out of the room.

Mona stood where he had left her, a pulse throbbing in her body like a tiny hammer, the blood burning in her cheeks. She must be mad, she told herself, or unsettled by the heat. She brushed the heavy hair away from her forehead and in doing so looked in the glass.

'I look just the same as I did three months ago,' she told the reflection, 'yet so many things have happened. I'm married and settled down with the kindest husband in the world, and all the adventures are over. And I'm glad,' she added almost defiantly, as if the uttering of the words convinced herself.

That night Mona avoided Alec's eyes at dinner. They seemed to be mocking her composure, amused at her dignity as attentive hostess, teasing the seriousness of her discussion on household and estate plans with Peter.

It was a relief that he was leaving on the morrow. He was upsetting the peacefulness of her Eden, ruffling the waters of hitherto unstirred pools, breaking the silence of unviolated places. He tantalised her by his mysteries and unexpected moods. She never knew when he was serious or acting a part – he would turn anything into a jest yet be furious with a disconcerting suddenness if one laughed in the wrong place. Mona thought him incomprehensible and an irritant to her preconceived and formulated ideas. Alec had a way of arguing and coercing until a certain conviction was completely destroyed, leaving a blank. Like a naughty small boy he took a pleasure in destruction – but creation was a trouble unattempted.

After dinner they sat outside on the terrace, patching the stars appearing one by one until the skies were strewn like a glittering garment, listening to the owls hooting in the woods, and the thin high squeak of the bats, swirling, dipping, whirling with incredible rapidity as though on important errands. The men smoked in silence and Togs slept on Mona's lap. After a little while Alec rose and, without a word, walked through the long window into the darkness of the room behind them. He sat down at the piano and started to play Chopin's *Nocturnes*. It was the one thing needed to complete the perfection of the night, conjuring up dreams and longings too indefinite to formulate, yet wondrously sweet. To Peter the music spoke of Mona, and of her only, expressing in the liquid notes his love, telling in the harmonious melody of her beauty and precious qualities – but to Mona it brought a craving for heights too supreme for realisation. She was straining to reach a nameless goal, wanting it with an almost physical intensity. Alec, with his curious inconsistency, before the last quivering notes of the *Nocturne* died away, struck the first wailing chords of a Hungarian Death Dance, in which the agony of the body as it dies changes to a note of supreme exultation at the release of the soul, ending with the triumphant cry of one who has attained his desire.

The strange rendering of the curious subject made Mona somehow uneasy that Alec was talking to her through the music was an idea that persisted. The first awakening movements of the soul, growing with a knowledge of its freedom into a passionate theme, sensuous with the delight of its happiness, drunk with the attainment of desires long craved for yet denied. Uncertainty of her own emotions made Mona feel a stranger to herself. The music was upsetting her – she felt as though it was forcing an unwelcome knowledge upon her, dragging her from dreams to face an unpleasant truth, making her listen against her will. On an impulse Mona pushed her chair nearer to Peter's – dear Peter, protective and secure. She put out her hand and held his.

CHAPTER X

June, July, August, September, October! Five months!

Mona yawned, then looked at her engagement calendar and yawned again. She was frankly, unashamedly and terribly bored. They had spent the whole of August and September in Scotland, staying for some of the time with friends and the rest on Peter's moor with just a few "perfect" shots for company, and with nothing to do but to think of sport from early in the morning when one started for the butts, till nightfall when one discussed every drive in detail. Mona had adored the heather-scented moors, stretching away into the grey distance, rising to great heights, the heavy sky, sometimes touching their gaunt tops, veiling their hardness in a soft mist. The wide, windswept spaces held a charm she had never experienced before, an attraction of freedom, untrammelled, unfettered.

Yet to Mona Scotland was a land of sadness, of a sorrow too deep for tears. The spirit of a woman facing the world with indomitable courage, scorning help or sympathy, yet hiding a tragedy in the depths of her heart.

About the second week in October they returned to Taylsea. The woods were all golden-brown save for the dark patches of fir and pine trees, the flowers in the gardens were dead, and the mists in the valley chill and damp. The cold winds whistled round the house, making the old oak creak ominously, blowing down the wide chimneys and rattling the ancient windows. It made Mona feel she was the only alive thing in the whole house. The atmosphere of past generations oppressed her like their pictures round the walls, dark with age. Her nerves were all on edge. She wanted to scream at them, to hurl abuse at their inanimateness, to cry, "I am alive, alive, *alive!*"

Peter wanted to hunt, or she would have asked him to take her abroad. The packs around them were not first class, but Peter believed in supporting his own county and refused to rent a hunting-box in a better centre. Mona in some ways was only too pleased not to have to face the strangeness of a fashionable hunting crowd, the hard-riding cocktail-drinking women alternating with the affected scandal-creating species. Yet she longed for companions. The neighbours around Taylsea were few and comparatively dull. They were either too overawed by the new Marchioness to be interesting, or absolutely unintelligent and dull.

Mona wrote to Sally asking her to come and stay indefinitely. She received an answer that made her boredom the more acute.

'Darling, I really can't get away from town just now. Everything is so much fun and I'm really having a wonderful time. I've got three new young men! And we're going to have a series of small dances this winter. I do wish you were here, Mona dear. I miss you horribly. Charles has had four different affaires *in the last month. Thank goodness, I have quite got over that. Do write darling.*

In great haste,

Sally.'

Sally of the broken heart and ruined life seemed to have disappeared with the cocoon that had fallen from the spirit of this carefree butterfly, fluttering in the sun, and even laughing at what had been herself. Frivolous but content! And suddenly Mona longed for the pavements and noise of London, the hectic glee of empty-headed youth turning over the husks in the dustbin of pleasure. The countryside, dreary in the greyness of the passing day, portrayed her own life, the monotony, the unrelieved drabness of the daily round, the common task, the abject boredom of a life without sunshine and shadow. It was an unfair addition of her existence, but at the moment her perspective was distorted, her feelings those of youth with unsatisfied red blood demanding an outlet. Mona even craved a row as a relief in the general unvarying calmness, but Peter was an impossible person to quarrel with. Arguments simply left him unmoved, and he made allowances for irritableness with a disarming sweetness impossible to combat. If only he would lose his temper, be brutal or abusive, Mona felt she would adore him. The eternal considerateness and kindness towards her simply rasped on her nerves. And yet she loved him – yes, with the affection of a child for a guardian. There was no passion for Peter the lover – there were no heart-breaking thrills in their companionship. Suddenly Mona realised that she was missing something, that marriage should mean more than friendship and mere bodily contact. She wanted to awaken from the drowsiness of this uneventful existence into a life of emotion, possibilities, sensations. Even a spice of danger was an attraction.

"I want to live," she said half-aloud, and with a nervous movement knocked a tiny Dresden china ornament off her writing-table on to the floor. It smashed into a thousand pieces, shattering the silence with a tinkling crash.

As she stared at her handiwork, the door opened and Peter came in, having been exercising the horses. He was in riding clothes, looking splendidly healthy, his brown face glowing, his eyes smiling for his wife. He saw the broken fragments on the polished floor.

"Oh, darling, what a pity! Was it an accident?"

"No." The answer was sharply unresponsive.

Peter looked surprised for a fleeting second, then changed the subject.

"Mrs. Holden has asked us over to dine tonight. Would you like to go?"

"Ten miles' drive for a bad dinner and a game of very indifferent bridge! Do you want to go?"

Peter hesitated before he answered.

"Not awfully, darling. But I don't want to offend them. I'm afraid it's rather a duty."

"Duty! Duty! Duty! I'm sick of the word. Do let's do something pleasant for once because we want to." Then, as she glanced at Peter's hurt face, her mood changed with bewildering rapidity. "I'm sorry, Peter dear. I'm a perfect beast. Don't take any notice of me. Of course we'll go." She silenced his protests with a smiling gesture. "I want to, really. Accept prettily for me." She pressed a quick kiss on his cheek in passing and ran out of the room.

That evening Peter saw a strange Mona, a creature of a thousand graces, coquetteries, affectations, attractive with a brilliance unlike the quiet flinging girl he had known for the last five months. A dress of shimmering silver made her look older than usual, but gave her a new and subtle charm, a maturity to her slimness, a sensuousness to every movement. The Holdens' party, consisting of about eight neighbours, was dull as Mona had predicted, but ten minutes after her arrival she awoke it to unimagined hilarity, thawing the stiffness of best behaviour and best clothes suffused by country people who dine out perhaps half a dozen times in the year and the slight awe with which they regarded this dazzling apparition, whose pale face and wonderful dress against their weather-beaten complexions and tasteless garments made her seem an inhabitant from another world.

Somerset is too far from London to have the usual clientele of social notabilities who live half the year in town and the other half in the country. Even the tourist and tripper is "of the land," moving from north to south and east to west, but nevertheless a son of "Zummerzet".

The guests at the Holdens' were typical west-country folk, ignorant of the latest scandal, neither knowing nor caring about the most recent plays or fashionable dancing haunts, but interested in their farms, estates and woodlands, comparing results with their neighbours, proud as a woman with a new jewel if they picked up a bargain at the local horse fair, or won a prize at a pig show in the next village. The women were real companions, mates to their husbands in the true sense of the word, the lives bound together by common interests, mutual desires and ambitions, breeding sturdy children to be healthy labouring men and women, fine citizens for the Great Empire.

Mona opened secret wells of humour in their methodical brains. They expanded under her charms. She radiated until they found themselves uttering sparkling witticisms, utterly unlike anything they had imagined themselves capable of conceiving. It is the touch of true genius in a special entertainer to cause others to reflect brilliance, believing it to be their own light.

After dinner the green tables invited bridge with the monotony of unvarying custom, but the packs of cards remained unopened, the pads and pencils unused. For Mona, at her hostess's invitation, went to the piano and started to sing. To Peter this was an unknown talent. He was ignorant that she had studied under one of the best masters in Paris and that her grandmother, the Countess of Templedon, had insisted on her often performing in the holidays so as to lose the paralysing shyness created by a critical audience. Mona had always hated what she called "showing off", and it had never occurred to her to talk of her accomplishments to Peter. Innately modest about herself, she despised her voice as too small to be effective or to be worthy of being labelled 'good'. She did not realise that her sweet low tones were infinitely more attractive in a drawing-room than the confined screech of an opera singer. Tonight, feeling that anything was better than the dreariness of bad bridge with the points at a shilling a hundred, she determined to avoid it at all costs.

She began by singing a quaint Irish folk-song, then, encouraged by the applause, she sang a little French sonnet set to the music of an ancient minuet – then, looking at the solemn faces around her, she broke into the latest American Blues. For a moment her audience merely looked surprised. The dance had not penetrated to their local Hunt ball or the few dances they attended. It was only "a name", read of in the Sunday papers, where it was apparently a bone in the throat of bishops and ecclesiastics, or was enthusiastically supported by short, argumentative letters from "A Keen Dancer", or "Rejuvenated Middle Age". Mona had chosen a ditty entitled *Dancing Dan.* It told of a dancing *Sheikh* who could make any girl love him for his wonderful feet. The tune began to fascinate with its lazy, movement-compelling time. Almost imperceptibly and quite unconsciously, the shoulders of the listeners started to sway and their faces lightened with laughter as "he has more women than

Wrigley has gum, that handsome Dancing Dan" finished the history of the gentleman.

"Bravo!"

"Encore!"

"Another one, please."

"Do go on."

Was this the sticky conventional dinner party?

Mona gave them another. *"Who is the meanest girl – in town? Josephine!"* and many more. By the end of the evening they had their favourites again and again, joining in the choruses, beating time with their hands and feet, humming verses, till at last Mona was too tired to go on, rising and departing amidst cries of regret and disappointment.

Driving home Peter was strangely quiet, listening to Mona's cheerful chatter and comments on the evening but answering her in monosyllables only. He acquiesced without argument, but as though he had anticipated the possibility when Mona said, as they neared home,

"I want to go up to town tomorrow for a few nights. Do you mind, Peter dear?"

CHAPTER XI

London! Dirty streets and muddy pavements, dingy houses, bare trees and a dark grey sky over all, the rattling red buses, the slowly-moving taxis, the loitering passers-by. London never seems to be in a hurry. She moves deliberately like a rather pompous dowager walking across a room, waggling a little with self-importance, considering her dignity.

Yet it was the joy of homecoming to see it all again.

Even the suburbs were interesting, the rows of dilapidated villas whose back gardens, in truth but a courtesy term, invariably contain laundry and an aerial. With them it is apparently always "washing-day." It must be a Herculean task, for as each train passes innumerable smuts are left behind. And by the end of the day the once-clean linen must resemble the reputation of one of those brave spirits who brave the divorce courts. The usual collection of small children waved excitedly as each train passed. As they can avail themselves of this amusement every ten minutes of the day, it is surprising that they do not tire. But no! Always the grubby hands are raised in welcome, and one suspects the open mouths denote cheers. How we should miss them if one day they bored of this impartial hospitality! How desolate, how lonely, to enter the great capital without a greeting from those fluttering fingers, a smile from those smutty faces.

Mona decided to stay at Belgrave Square. Peter had never exercised his right to the house in Lancaster Gate after the Duchess died, and Alec reigned there undisputed. Peter had a small flat in Mount Street, but it had been shut up since his marriage and Mona hesitated to face the dreariness of dismantled rooms and the attentions of an ancient caretaker.

Lady Vivien was delighted to see her. A married daughter, especially a Marchioness, was a desirable attainment. Mona found nothing changed. Even her bedroom and *boudoir* were untouched. She might never have been away.

"How long can you stay with us, dearest?" her mother asked, sandwiching the question between a description of a new dress and the story of a friend's divorce.

"I don't know. A day or two," Mona had answered vaguely.

She had first of all said a week to Peter – then as she was leaving, compunction overcame her. He had seemed so wistful at her departure and she had clung to him for one moment in the privacy of an empty railway carriage.

"I'll come back terribly quickly, Peter dear. I just want to buy a new hat."

Only afterwards the pathetic bitterness in his smile had struck her, and she had wondered. It never occurred to Peter to accompany her – he knew intuitively that Mona wanted to be alone. And although he hated her going, he counted his own feelings too little to let them interfere with any desire of hers.

Only as the train steamed out of the station and Mona had a last glimpse of Peter and Togs waving farewell, did she regret her hasty decision and its fulfilment. She wanted to jump out of the train and go back to them, back to the security of the last five months. Then, in spite of her refusal to face or believe it, youth began to rejoice at the unexpected freedom and in anticipation of adventures ahead.

Lady Vivien was having a party that night and begged Mona not to go out. Mona, who had planned a visit to a theatre with Sally, hesitated, then was persuaded. She shopped most of the afternoon. After being buried alive for five months everything she wore seemed old-fashioned and unsmart. The shops held entrancing treasures, but after a quiet tea Mona went to the cinema, feeling like a truant from school, a nursemaid on an afternoon out. The drama was violently sensational enough to thrill her, and the slapstick comedies were inordinately amusing for one who had almost forgotten how to laugh at nonsense. Even the music pleased and she returned to Belgrave Square after the dressing-gong had sounded, and Annette was wondering what accident could have befallen her.

Laid out on the bed was a dress of pale yellow and gold lace, a beautiful garment that made Mona slim with the youthful freshness of spring sunshine. Almost shamefacedly she produced, the spoil of the afternoon and unpacked it. A wonderful dress of deep red, like a huge drop of blood fell from the unfolding layers of white paper. She put it on, then surveyed herself in the glass and found that it portrayed to perfection her new mood – a slight recklessness, a hungry desire to live. The whiteness of her arms and shoulders gleamed through the chiffon and her bare back gave whole effect a sophisticated look against the darkness of her hair and the brightness of her eyes. For the first time in her life she reddened her lips and it made the brilliance of her colouring the more striking.

The man who took her down to dinner flirted through the courses, and Mona found herself adept at the strange language – the usual patter, obvious compliments in every sentence, the inability to keep the conversation from becoming personal.

"You remind me of a girl I knew once, oh, she was very beautiful ... your hair is so wonderful – it's a public shame it should be hidden, how long is it down? ... Peter? Who is Peter? your husband! What has he done to deserve such luck?

And, "A grass widow ... only for a night or so ... my eyes? Oh, no, they are very ordinary. This dress! I'm glad you like it, I wasn't quite sure…"

On and on – squirrels in a revolving cage.

Afterwards a good many people came in to dance, important, notorious, intelligent people with famous names. Yet none were so remarkable to the onlooker as the dark girl in the red dress moving like a flame, flickering about the room like a little tongue of fire.

The men fought among themselves for her dances and, during one half-amused, half-serious scrap, when two competitors claimed the same dance, she suddenly found herself in the arms of a stranger who merely remarked,

"Well, dance with me while they are arguing," and propelled her round the room. He was a nice-looking boy of about twenty-two or three and Mona responded to the laughter in his mischievous blue eyes.

"I think this is a rotten show," he said after they had danced several encores. "Let's go on to a club."

Mona was amused. He evidently had no idea who she was, but it was not surprising, as few people recognised her as Lady Vivien's daughter, and though the newspapers had printed a thousand photographs of "the beautiful young Marchioness of Leadenhall" their reproductions were notably lifeless.

"It's too late," she said. "They shut about half-past twelve or one o'clock."

"Oh, do they?" he interrupted. "I'll take you to one that goes on till five. Do come."

"I wonder if I dare," she hesitated.

"To wonder is human, to dare divine," he misquoted.

Mona laughed and was lost.

"All right. I'll come for a little while."

"That's marvellous! I knew you were divine."

"If I'm caught, I shall be propelled forcibly from Olympus," Mona retorted.

"Oh, you won't be!" he replied. "Blessed is he that can escape detection."

"Your metaphors are too mixed for my intelligence," smiled Mona.

"And your beauty too dazzling for mine," was the quick reply.

Still buffooning they hurried downstairs and into a taxi, Mona snatching up a shawl covered in heavy Chinese embroidery and wrapping it round her. Like two children on an adventure into the realms of imagination they watched the lights of Piccadilly flashing past, the blazing electric signs, like twinkling fairy lights shining first here, then there, multi-coloured and sparkling. Just before the Circus they plunged into a labyrinth of dark streets, the houses irregular and misshapen like the worn-down heels of a row of shoes beneath the dressing-table of a *fille de pavé*. In a moment, however, they drew up before a sinister building in a narrow alley. Shuttered and barred, it appeared deserted save for a commissionaire outside in blue and gold. They entered first a minute hall with a hatch on one side through which there appeared a head.

“Members?” enquired the head, its mouth full of a half-consumed sandwich.

“One and a guest,” replied Mona’s escort.

The head then produced from the depths of its dugout a book to be signed. Mona looked with interest to see what name he would give her.

“Miss Sylvia Scarlett,” he wrote.

“Shades of Compton Mackenzie!” laughed Mona, and looked quickly for his signature, but, with a little smile at her curiosity, he scribbled down some unintelligible initials only.

“Allons, Sylvia,” he said, and a door opened for them in the wall.

A long low room had a raised platform at the far end large enough to hold a piano, drum, drummer and a saxophonist. There were two or three tables near the door and the remaining few feet of space was crowded with dancers, swaying rather than moving, obeying the music as a menagerie obeys the crack of the circus ringmaster’s whip, their faces intent and solemn.

“Where would you like to sit?”

“Anywhere,” Mona answered vaguely. “But there doesn’t seem much room.”

Her partner led the way through a small opening near the band and, descending a few steps, Mona found herself in a sitting-out room. Low sofas and small tables were arranged round a quaint fountain in the centre, and red lights, discreetly shaded, cast a seductive sensuous glow on the whispering couples around. A hardly suitable atmosphere for a respectably married woman, thought Mona with a little twinge of conscience.

"Can't we find a table where we can watch the dancers?" she asked.

"Discretion, although the better part of valour, is sometimes cowardice," teased her companion guessing her preference for the brighter lights of the ballroom.

"I merely look before I leap," she retorted.

"And then don't! Stung again!" Laughing, he led her back and they found a small table and two chairs next the band, arranged in an alcove that was only a crevice in the wall. They danced two or three times and then Mona craved a rest. The heat and the close proximity of the dancers were overwhelming.

"Tell me who all the celebrities are," she commanded, glancing round at the fashionably dressed *bien-soignées* women with their immaculate escorts. Her companion nodded to two or three people before he spoke.

"It's the usual crowd of social notabilities who will be nonentities tomorrow," he began.

"But I'm a country cousin," Mona replied. "Who is the girl in black with the rather dissipated old man?"

"Oh, that's Clare Thishold, Lord Delton's daughter, you know, ran away with her father's chauffeur. Not that he minded that – only she took the car, too."

"Is that the gentleman in question?"

"Oh Lord, no, she left him after the first hundred miles or so. That's Lord Cavington, most awful blighter. His wife's charming but refuses to divorce him. There's the famous Flavita Puttio, Ostirsky's model. Personally, I think she's hideous."

"She looks so terribly wicked," said Mona as the tall girl danced past them, her black hair greased sleek to her head, long jade earrings touching her naked shoulders, and with heavily pencilled eyes slanting above a large crimson mouth.

"She is wickedly dull," was the criticism. "Ostirsky picked her up in the gutter somewhere and as she is totally uneducated and too unintelligent to be an amusing Cockney, he merely dressed her up and told her to be silent. Result – she is the rage, asked everywhere, and people find her delightfully mysterious."

"I think you are very scathing," said Mona. "Now *there's* a pretty girl," she added, pointing.

Her companion went into fits of laughter.

"She would be pleased," he guffawed. "That's Peggy More and she's sixty-nine!"

"Oh, but it's impossible! "cried Mona.

"She's had her face cut, monkey-glanded, or something. It's all right, only she daren't smile in case it cracks."

"How pathetic! I do hope I shan't want to do that when I get old."

"I don't think you will ever get old," he said insistently. "In fact, I believe you do not exist at all. You are a marvellous dream that will fade in the daylight."

"But even dreams must fade to somewhere – the land of rest for dreams, or the workhouse of unemployed fantasies."

"I'm afraid you will never be unemployed. I don't think you will ever be allowed a rest."

The atmosphere and lazy haunting music was soothing Mona into the flirtation, half-serious, half-joking. The youthfulness of her partner and the compelling attraction of his obvious admiration and caressing tones, made her feel like a cat who purrs in the warmth of a fire. She could not have snubbed him, and at the moment she would have led him on whatever he had said and almost in spite of herself.

"I think you are trying to pay compliments," she told him with a little flickering look. "I hate insincerity."

"Insincerity!" he repeated, intoning the word incredulously. "Shall I be really sincere, your adorable dream-child?" He bent towards her so near that she could feel his breath on her neck and was conscious of his eyes compelling her look at him. Very slowly she started to move her head so that in a moment, wordlessly, she would answer his question, acquiesce with a glance.

Suddenly her intention was arrested. There was a pause in the dancing. With a little shiver of material awakening she looked across the room, for, standing in the doorway, surprise, incredulity mingling in his face with a look Mona interpreted as a strange anger, was Alec.

CHAPTER XII

Mona's first impulse was flight, her second surprise at the thought. For why should she fly from Alec? All the same, she felt strangely perturbed at seeing him, and the colour crept slowly into her cheeks. Then, angry at her own feelings, she bowed gracefully and turned again to her companion, but for a moment he was interested in her diversion.

"Do you know Alec Gordon well?" he asked.

"Fairly well," Mona answered constrainedly.

"I think he is very nice."

"So do most women!" was the dry answer. "I hear…"

But the scandal went unspoken, for Alec, entirely unconcerned by Mona's cool bow, elbowed his way to her side.

"By all that's holy, Mona, what are you doing here?" he asked, adding, "Hello, Cathcart!" to her companion.

"I'm staying with my mother for a few days. I got up today," said Mona meekly, feeling like a schoolgirl caught out of bounds by a strict governess.

"Will you dance this with me? You don't mind, do you, old man?" This to her partner, who was bound to give his consent with the best grace he could muster.

"And he has more women than Wrigley has gum," yelled the band, and Mona wondered if it was true about Alec as he propelled her through the crowd of 'blueing' couples.

'He dances well,' was her thought, and she looked up at him with a little smile that turned to consternation as she saw his face.

"Why didn't you let me know you were in town?" he enquired almost fiercely.

"I never thought of it," she faltered. "I only came up today and Mother had a deadly party, so Mr... the man I was with, brought me on here."

"Cathcart's a fool," said Alec sharply, "and you have no right to be here at all!"

The authority in his tone aroused Mona's pride. No one could be allowed to talk to her like that.

"I can go where I like," she retorted, then gasped, for Alec tightened his hold until she was almost breathless, then answered her grimly,

"Not unless I am with you, Undine."

She was too surprised and bruised by his violence to answer. There must be a queer streak of cruelty in him, she thought, and questioned for the first time if the hardness of his jaw were not brutality rather than willpower and determination. As though he had punished her and been thereby appeased to forgiveness, Alec's mood changed and his deep voice held the well-remembered mocking note, although his dark eyes still kept their unfathomable gaze.

"A new Undine," he said, "not so mysterious and intangible as the dream princess of moonlit nights and hazy summer days. Are you tasting the forbidden fruits of mortality, Undine?"

The caressing quality of his last words made Mona thrill with the same disconcerting uncertainty as she had last seen him, almost forgotten in the last months until this moment, which found her unprepared and helpless in the seduction of the night and the portentous atmosphere.

"Only admiring them from afar," she answered, steadying her voice against the little waves of warmth stealing into her throat, almost seeming to choke her.

"And envying the consumers?" he questioned. "Poor little Eve still hesitating to pluck the apple yet too fascinated to refuse herself the pleasure of looking at it! You will take it in the end."

He spoke seriously and quite unreasonably. Mona found herself answering him in the same vein.

"No, I shan't, Alec. I am even safe from the temptation." It was a challenge.

"Are you?" Alec questioned, an odd smile flickering in his eyes. His hold tightened and doubt crept into Mona's mind. She wanted to hurl defiance in his face, laugh light-heartedly at her fears and his insinuations, and slip away to security – yet she could not. She was humiliatingly certain of the impossibility. She looked away from Alec and lied courageously.

"Quite safe." Yet the words lacked assurance and Alec's reply was disconcerting.

"Poor little dreamer fighting reality."

He was too intuitive for her peace of mind and, like a bird fluttering against the bars, she tried to escape from the web which seemed to be encircling her.

"I must go back to my partner, Alec."

"I can't let you go yet, Undine. I want to talk to you. Look here, it's quite early." He produced a flat platinum watch from his waistcoat pocket. "Two-thirty. Let Cathcart take you home now and I'll call for you at Belgrave Square in a quarter of an hour. I won't keep you out late, really ... Undine, *please.*"

How could she resist Alec when he pleaded? Was it his French blood that made him the more virile than other men and made his love-making more intense, his desires more forceful?

"You want to come, Undine! Why deny yourself a harmless pleasure?" He watched her eyelids flutter, the soft beat of the pulse in her white throat. "Darling, *please.*"

What harm could there be in it? Mona questioned her conscience. Just a few minutes with her brother-in-law – after all, what was she frightened of?

"All right, Alec." She surrendered and saw the triumph blaze into his eyes.

"Bless you."

Cathcart was approaching them and without another word Alec disappeared into the crowd

"Will you take me home?" said Mona sweetly.

"Must you go so soon? How sickening!" he said boyishly.

Mona was rather silent driving home, but her companion talked volubly all the way. He discovered who she was and was very apologetic at having abused her mother's dance.

"But it's quite all right," Mona assured him. "I always hate them myself." She thanked him for the delightful evening and he begged to see her again for lunch, tea, or dinner tomorrow, any time she could manage. She chose tea and he was delighted.

"Claridge's at four-thirty," he instructed. "Goodnight, dream lady."

"Good night, Cavalier."

The taxi drove off. Mona glanced at the hall clock. There were five minutes to wait before Alec arrived. She ran upstairs to her room, fire cast flickering shadows on the ceiling and shone on her nightgown spread on a chair. Her fur-trimmed slippers were waiting in front of it.

She switched on the lights and examined herself in the glass of her dressing-table. Was this vision of sparkling eyes, flushed cheeks and parted red mouth really herself? Where was the pale ethereal face of Madonna-like severity with, dreaming eyes gazing into a spirit world of unreality?

From a wardrobe she took a coat of soft sable, for the night was cold, and the deep fur collar framed her face and fell open to accentuate the smallness of her proportions until she appeared more than ever like a little vivid flame caught for a moment in a web of shadows.

Three minutes more! Why did she feel so strangely excited, her heart beating like a little hammer – *throb, throb, throb*.

It reminded her somehow of the night she had married, how she had waited in the strange hotel bedroom after Annette had left her, listening to Peter's movements in the dressing-room next door, the shutting of drawers, the rattle of dressing-table things, the splash of water in his basin, and all the time her heart had beat with sickening intensity. She had been too nervous to move across the room and get into bed – she had just sat, listening and listening, until Peter had knocked at the door, and then all the pulses in her body had given a tremendous jump and seemed to drain away, leaving a quivering emptiness.

"Come in!" Her voice had seemed like a stranger's, faint and quavering.

And Peter had entered, dear Peter, looking so young and unfrightening in his blue dressing-gown, his hair not so severely sleek as usual, and he had smiled, his familiar kind smile.

But Mona had still sat paralysed, clutching the table in front of her with desperate hands, her face white against the dark masses of unbound hair. With fascinated eyes she watched Peter walk across the room towards her, his feet soundless on the heavy carpet.

"Shall I carry you to bed, darling?" It the dear, steady, grave voice of the Peter who taken her away from the horrors of the dance and the nameless fears that Sally had conjured up. Suddenly her muscles had relaxed and Mona lifted soft arms to her husband's neck like unhappy child.

"Peter, Peter!"

And he held her tightly, securely, soothingly, while she cried on his shoulder, just kissing away the softness of her hair and letting her wash away her last doubts and fears, until she had raised a pale face to be kissed, the dark lashes wet, but her mouth quivering in an April smile.

Mona pulled up her thoughts with a little jerk. Why was she thinking about this now? Peter trusted her – but was she to be trusted? With a little flash her conscience shot the question into her brain. She had done nothing wrong tonight, she argued defiantly. Except feel wrong, was the answer.

'But I can't help it,' she told herself helplessly. 'Then don't run into danger!'

Into danger? Was Alec dangerous? Even as she asked the question she heard his car rounding the corner of the square, heard his Claxon awakening the darkness, listened to the purr of his engine as he drew up outside the front door. Her heart throbbing, she pulled on her coat, then turned to extinguish the lights. A photograph by her bedside caught her eyes, only a snapshot, but of Peter and

Togs taken in the sunshine at Taylsea. Peter smiling with happiness, serene contentment in his face.

She must not go. The Claxon skreeled again. Alec was getting impatient.

"Oh, Peter, *Peter!*" Mona threw herself on the bed, covering her ears to drown the sound.

Below Alec swore softly at the locked door.

CHAPTER XIII

In the clear light of the morning Mona laughed at herself. Her fears seemed distorted, exaggerated and absurd, so when Alec rang up and asked her to have tea with him, she assented readily, chucking Mr. Cathcart without a second thought.

She wrote to Peter, an affectionate letter, telling him of her arrival and her mother's party. She even mentioned going on to a club and that Alec was there. After all, she had nothing tangible to hide from Peter, only the chaotic muddle of her feelings.

Alec called for her about four o'clock in his car and complimented her on her appearance. A long coat of deep green had a collar of dark fur, which was turned up round a tiny hat of the same colour.

"You are elusive again today, Undine," said Alec. "I shall have to do something about it," and he drove to Solomon's, the florist, whose beflowered windows attract the Piccadilly passers-by.

Alec disappeared into the shop, leaving Mona outside, and after a moment returned with a bunch of deep red carnations.

Mona pinned them on to her coat.

"They are perfectly lovely," she thanked him.

"Like you. Undine. Red roses are supposed to represent passion and true love, but for you they are too transparent, their petals unfolding to reveal the centre, to surrender as it were with one gesture, whole-heartedly, irrevocably – but in a carnation the petals, like a hundred different words, hide the anther, the heart and axis of the emotions, distracting the attention of the explorer with the beauty of each brilliant curve or curling edge."

"Are my words so incomprehensible?" said Mona, knowing he was referring to last night.

"Only tantalising," he replied, "but prolonged anticipation makes the attainment all the sweeter, Undine."

"If one attains," she evaded.

"Unattainable, like impossible, is a word created by the faint-hearted. Real determination never fails."

There was a serious depth underlying the surface lightness of his tone, and Mona, with a consciousness of thin ice, changed the subject abruptly.

"Where are we going to have tea?"

"At Lancaster Gate," he answered. "I want you to see the picture of my French ancestress again, by daylight this time."

Mona felt the blood rushing to her face. So Alec hadn't forgotten the kiss of their first meeting. They had never referred to it, and she hoped it had escaped his memory. A *tête-à-tête* with Alec was not at all the sort of tea she had planned. It was a situation too insecure for pleasure. She preferred the noise and movement of a hotel, with plenty of distraction around. But she had no reasonable excuse for refusal. Peter had often said she must go and see the treasures at Lancaster Gate, the valuable pictures, all heirlooms, and a unique collection of snuff-boxes left to Alec by his French grandfather.

One thing at the moment was really important. Alec must not perceive that she was worried or notice any embarrassment. As naturally as possible, with a touch of coolness in her voice, she answered him.

"I'll love to see it again. I'm ashamed to say I know none of the family perquisites when people talk of the marvels of the Gordon collection."

"Another mood, Undine?"

And Mona flushed. To snub him was impossible. On arrival he led her into the hall and she saw at once the wonderful ivory carvings she had noticed on her first visit.

"They are all Chinese," Alec said, "and stolen from the Emperor's palace by the third Marquis. There is a story that he even made love to the Empress herself during his efforts to procure them."

She loved the quaint grotesque figures, each intricate contortion perfect in every detail, but life, or the loss of it, would have been a big price to pay for the possession of mere ornaments.

The dining-room was hung with the inimitable art of Gainsborough, Rembrandt, Rubens, and one priceless Cuyp, the masts of a resting fishing fleet silhouetted against the setting sun. A small sitting room held the Primitives, beautiful in their stiff severity and deep colouring, their carved frames, mostly gilt, were a fitting setting for such valuable jewels.

"And now for tea," said Alec, and led Mona upstairs to the well-remembered drawing-room. A log fire was blazing in the fireplace and above it hung the picture of the beautiful Marquise. The silver kettle was boiling on the table strewn with a luxurious tea and covered with a cloth of beautiful old English embroidery and fine crocheted lace.

Mona slipped out of her heavy coat and revealed a dress coloured to match, made in one of her favourite materials, falling in the soft folds that reminded Alec of the robes of the gentle Madonna they had been looking at downstairs.

"Take off your hat," Alec pleaded. "I want to pretend you belong here. Please, Undine."

Weakly and half-angry with her own compliance, Mona did as he asked and, avoiding his eyes, which held a strange hunger, she made the tea and poured it out into cups of delicate old Worcester china.

"Tell me what you have been doing since you came down to stay with us in July, Alec," she asked, leaning back in her chair, her head against a cushion of faded crimson velvet.

"Stealing fruit from other people's orchards," was the enigmatic reply.

'Women,' thought Mona, and was vaguely hurt.

"Was it worth the risk of detection?" she queried.

"The risk is the only enjoyable part. 'Stolen fruits are the sweetest' in reality refers to the act of stealing, not to the fruit, which is generally inferior."

"How cynical!" cried Mona. "I thought you enjoyed the 'living' of your life."

"I hate killing time," was the irrelevant reply.

"Then why..." But Mona stopped. Alec was looking at her in an odd way, his body and his muscles tightened as though he were holding himself in check by sheer force of willpower.

His eyes, blazing with concentrated passion, were compellingly magnetic.

Without conscious thought she rose, only aware of the wave of emotion sweeping over her. She felt herself drawn towards him, everything, save a desire too strong to be denied, dissolving into oblivion. An odd flame seemed to flicker inside her, devouring the very breath of her body. Her eyes felt weighted and heavy, yet she could not separate their gaze from his. For a moment she stood palpitating, a frightened nymph, the green dress clinging around her yet seeming to hide nothing of the primitive nakedness she felt in her first encounter with passion.

With a single feline movement Alec sprang up and took her in his arms. Her head fell against his shoulder and, with a muttered sound, half-groan, half-cry of triumph as of a hunter with his prey, he pressed his mouth to hers.

A minute, an hour, a year – how long had it been?

Mona hid her face against Alec's shoulder. In that long kiss she had awakened from girlhood for the first time. Although physically a married woman, she was mentally virginal. Bodily contact had been unreal, a demonstration, necessary and natural because Peter was her husband, but arousing no answering affection in herself. She had expelled Nature with a pitchfork, to be punished now with a return of emotions and feelings beyond anything she had imagined or fled from.

For the moment she was too dazed and bewildered to analyse her feelings, the pulsing of her nerves, the rise and fall of her breath, the flutter of shy eyelids, told of the tumult within, of the red blood flowing for the first time through the beautiful body. She only knew it was Heaven to be in Alec's arms, to listen to his whispered endearments. Her marriage ties were forgotten in this seduction from dreams to a reality far more intangible.

"Darling! My God, how beautiful you are!" Alec bent to kiss her neck.

She quivered at his touch, then pushed him away, twisting from his hold.

"Oh, Alec," she said, with a little break in her voice. "What have we done?"

"Been frank with ourselves at last," he answered caressingly. "My Undine, don't go away!"

But she evaded his outstretched arms.

"Peter," she faltered.

"God!" Alec sank into the armchair, his brows knit together. "Do you imagine I haven't thought of it all? Do you think it was easy to stay away from you these last months, which seemed years?"

"I didn't know." It was almost a cry from Mona.

"You did!" Fiercely Alec shattered the sanctuary of excuses she was building. "You are mine, and you knew it, knew it the last day I saw you in Taylsea when you trembled as I held you."

He crossed to her side.

"Undine, darling, aren't you going to tell me you care a tiny bit?"

"Oh, I do, I do!" For a moment he held her to him, then, without kissing her, he picked up her discarded coat.

"I'll take you home, darling. If you stay now, I shall never let you go." There was raw passion in his voice, but Mona was not frightened. In the surrender of her emotional virginity she had lost the fear of primitiveness. Civilisation was but a thin coating after all.

He tucked her into the car, fussing the rug around her knees with all the care of Peter. They were very alike, she thought with a strange pain in her heart. Yet she had married the wrong one. But had she? The question surprised her. One never connected Alec with marriage. He was too aesthetic, too artistic, for the wear and tear of every day. As the perfect lover he must always be staged in the spotlights, with no distracting backgrounds. The attraction of broken sentences, half-finished conversations, interrupted whispers would be void without the disturbances that leave one anticipating.

"Stolen fruit!"

With a little sob Mona realised that Alec was playing an old game, familiar through repetition. Then in the darkness of the car she felt his hand feeling for hers and, obeying an undeniable impulse, she turned her face to his.

CHAPTER XIV

"God damn!" Alec swore softly – then the Gordon temper made him take up the whisky and soda from the small table beside him and hurl it at the opposite wall. The cut-glass tumbler crashed into a thousand pieces while the liquid made a dark stain on the blue carpet.

Mona had run away – flown back to security in the shape of Peter. She was to have dined with Alec at the Berkeley and he was waiting now till the hands on the clock pointed to a quarter-past eight before he started off to fetch her. And while he waited, she had fled, leaving only a little note, brief with the cruelty of a few lines to an impetuous lover. There was no beginning, for Mona could not start with the irony of "Dear Alec", and her real feelings couldn't be translated into words.

'I am going home tonight by the eight o'clock express. Cowardly but ... bless you.

Mona.'

He could see her writing it while Annette packed, the determination in her little white face, the disappointed pain in her dear eyes.

"Cowardly but..." What was she going to say? Wise? It was certainly that. Brave? It was bravery to forswear one's own desires, to fight a strong inclination. God! It was millions of different things, but who cared? It was unkind, brutal, maddening, to leave him like this – wanting her beyond expression.

Had she any idea, he wondered, how tempting the elusiveness of her beauty was to a man of his temperament? The pale spiritual face that was but a frame for the wonderful eyes – eyes that saw through the commonplace without realising their perception. Nothing vulgar could come near to Mona – it shrivelled at birth. But evil was not so easily quelled. The greedy grasping fingers of hungry men, coveting a priceless jewel. How passionate she would be when fully awakened! The thought made the Latin blood throb in Alec's veins. He had but picked the lock of her prison. Would fickle Fate cast to him the lot of opening the door? It was his right! He denied the suggestion of chance. To win Mona he would defy the gods themselves. She was his by conquest, the spoils of his victory. For a moment he stood silent in the dimly-lit room, then it seemed as if a faint laugh reached his ears.

Furious, he scoffed at himself. Love had apparently upset his nerves. With a steady hand he poured himself another drink. With a mocking bow he toasted the picture of the smiling Marquise.

"A votre santé, Madame," he murmured. The drink calmed his anger. The clock on the mantelpiece chimed the half-hour. Where the hell was he to dine? If only Undine could be with him...

He must see her again. With another oath he went to his writing-table and commenced a letter to Peter.

*

"You're going home, you're going home, you're going home..." sang the wheels of the Bristol express.

Mona stirred uneasily in her corner of the carriage. Eight-thirty. Alec would just have been calling for her, the silver car purring outside the door, his top-hat at the angle she loved, the light shining on the immaculate white shirt and waistcoat, the flower in his buttonhole. Why did one remember the little things when one loved, rather than visualise the whole?

She had wired to Peter so that he would meet her. Once again he was to be a haven from the world, an inviolable sanctuary. They would have been at dinner now, the band playing dreamily in the distance, only the rose-lighted table between them, Alec watching her with dark eyes, perceiving every movement, each expression of her mood, saying...

Would they ever get there? She tried to read, but her brain refused to register what her eyes saw. The printed pages danced dizzily before her.

Dear Peter! Then, with a little shock of regarding a familiar object from another point of view, she realised that Peter could not be asked to give advice, that protection would have to be sought from him unawares. She was so used to thinking of Peter as a kind maternal guardian, always ready with sympathy and antidotes to every ill, that a secret ache he could not share seemed unnatural. For the first time she visualised Peter as a man with normal feelings, natural desires and jealousies. The latter was absurd. She couldn't imagine Peter angry. The Gordon scowl appeared sometimes if things went wrong, but Peter's muscles only tightened, his hands clenched, and then without a word the mood would pass and Peter was himself, suave, unruffled and smiling.

She must have dozed off, for she awoke with a start to find Annette collecting the hand luggage.

"Brees-tol – Brees-tol!" yelled the porters.

Among the hurrying passengers she saw Peter looking up and down anxiously, his face lighting as she waved.

"Hello, darling!" She was glad of the rushing crowd which excused a reply and prevented any affectionate demonstrations.

"The car is outside." They clambered over the bridge to the impressive entrance of Bristol Station, built on a hill, the drive up ending in a semicircle of buildings.

As she got in a small, excited bundle hurled itself upon her.

"Togs! Are you glad to see me then?" The wiggling squirming body was vaguely comforting.

Annette got into the back seat with the luggage and Mona sat beside Peter, who was driving. As they got out of the traffic of the city into the country lanes, he removed one hand from the wheel and took hers.

"I'm terribly glad you are back, darling," he said.

"Did you miss me?"

"Of course."

She knew he had, but Alec would have said far more. She stopped – why must she compare the two, and with a little effort she forced herself to sit nearer to Peter and be nice.

"I couldn't stay away any longer! "She felt, rather than saw, the gladness in his face. He kissed the tips of her fingers without taking his eyes from the road.

"It wasn't really very long." He was smiling.

Only one night! Was it possible? A whole lifetime of events had happened and yet only two days had passed on the calendar. In the distance she could see the lights of Taylsea Court – her Rhine-castle high above the snaring tempting river, the glittering mirages created by its swirling depths, dazzling, enticing. Safe behind the bars of respectability and love she would ignore them, shutting her ears to the siren music of rippling gurgles as it journeyed past her.

"I'm glad to be home," she said later, gazing out of her bedroom windows towards the hills, their dim outline showing against the dark starless sky. "Peter, Peter, don't let me go again!" It was a cry to convince herself rather than an appeal to him, for she wanted to go. It was almost a physical pain to wonder what Alec was doing at the moment. Only midnight, the dancing clubs and restaurants still blazing with light, couples moving lazily to the sensuous music, she might have been with Alec dancing with his arm round her...

"Do you know, I haven't kissed my prodigal wife yet?" asked Peter, disturbing her thoughts.

"Oh, Peter, I'm so tired." It was a quick instinct to refuse him. She regretted it a moment later.

"Poor darling! Hurry into bed. I'll call Annette." He dropped a light kiss on her forehead and left the room.

'Alec!' The ache in her heart was a tiny needle of pain, sharp and virulent.

She undressed mechanically without speaking – only when she was in bed and as Annette was leaving her, did she notice that Peter's pillow had been taken from the bed, leaving hers in solitary state.

"His Lordship is sleeping in his dressing-room as he has got to get up early to see about some ponies," Annette answered the question Mona's surprised face asked. "He thought perhaps you would sleep late and have a good night."

Dear, kind, considerate Peter. Gratefulness turned into doziness, and incredibly quickly Mona was asleep.

*

More stairs, leading upwards in a kind of never-ending crescendo. She was so tired, but she must go on, up, up, up. They grew darker every minute until she missed the step and nearly fell. *It* was just behind. She could hear the footsteps gather speed. Up, up, up. It was getting nearer, *nearer...* Her feet seemed weighted with lead, couldn't hurry. Would the stairs never end? There was salvation at the top, she knew that, only she could get there! She couldn't scream. Only a tiny breath came when she tried. *It* was almost touching her. One last effort, she felt *its* breath on her neck. Too late – *it* had caught her!

"Peter! Peter! *Peter!!!*"

And suddenly it was all right. Strong arms were holding her – someone was soothing her fear.

"Peter, don't let it, don't!"

"It's all right, darling, you're only dreaming.

She opened terrified eyes. Peter's face was close to hers, her arms were clasped convulsively round his neck.

"There, wake up, and see you are quite safe," he smiled.

"Am I?" Her voice still broke in a frightened sob, the room seemed full of dark shades. curtains moving slightly in the draught from the windows hid strange fantasies.

"Don't go away, Peter, please. I'm so frightened."

"I won't, darling. Don't worry." He got into bed. "Shall I get my pillow?"

"No, no, share mine." Feverishly she clutched him, the pursuing phantoms of her dream rising with her fear of being left alone.

The security of Peter being with her was very comforting, but Mona now felt strangely wide awake. She started to talk, and somehow the conversation veered round to her schooldays at the convent. In the darkness it was easy to tell Peter lots of things that the daylight made difficult. Little hopes and ambitions of growing girlhood, horrors of half-knowledge, the searching among whispered secrets, veiled insinuations, and literary lies for the real truth about life, withheld in distorted modesty from children instead of being taught them cleanly and healthily as the beauty of Nature.

Reminiscing for herself rather than Peter, Mona was startled when in a pause he suddenly broke the silence with a question.

"Mona darling, would you like to have a baby?"

A baby! She knew little about them, but the maternal instinct made her crave to mother something of her own, to feel a tiny warm body in her arms, to know that no one else could have her privileges with the living creation that would turn to her first ... but it would be Peter's too. How could she bear his child if she didn't love the father? Would it not only be unfair to him but also unfair to the baby – perhaps tainting its nature, embittering its life?

"No, Peter," she answered, and unaccountably burst into tears.

CHAPTER XV

Rain beating on the windows, rain splashing into the ever-widening puddles on the paths and saturated lawns, rain hiding the hills with a grey sheet, joining earth to sky in a monotonous line of drab sombreness. Only in Mona's heart lay the sunshine, the warmth and the light of it shining in her eyes as she moved about the house. Peter had frowned over his letters at breakfast.

"Alec wants us to put him up tonight and perhaps tomorrow. What a bore, darling! I wanted you all to myself."

But Mona had turned her head from him, busying herself in feeding the greedy Togs to hide the gladness that sprang with a faint colour to her face.

Alec was coming to see her! The thought sang a little tune in her ears and her pulses beat time with excited rapidity. There was so much to do – the joy of arranging his room herself, ruthlessly picking the best carnations in the conservatory to decorate his dressing-table, choosing with care a few interesting books for his bedside.

The day passed so quickly, the hours seeming to slip through her fingers like drops of water. She went up to dress for dinner early. Alec was sure to be late and she would hurry down to welcome him on arrival. Dressing took longer than she intended. It was so difficult to choose her most becoming gown. The room was littered with discarded garments and Annette was rapidly losing her temper before Mona finally decided. The choice was the colour of Parma violets, the upper part forming a coat of soft chiffon trimmed with silver ribbon and edged with chinchilla. It reflected in her eyes, making them seem purple, flecked with light like the centre of a pansy. Ready at last she went downstairs, noting with apprehension that a clock in the hall pointed the quarter to eight. What could have happened to Alec? Had there been an accident? She entered the sitting room, wondering apprehensively, in darkness save for the light from a huge log fire flickering on the furniture and among the old oak beams on the ceiling.

Mona felt for the lights and even as she did so found herself lifted off her feet by a figure that sprang from the shadows. Her heart gave one frightened leap, then before she felt his mouth on hers she knew whose arms held her, thrilled with the knowledge of his strength and loved the almost brutal roughness of his passion.

"Darling, how you frightened me!" How dear he was!

"And you are glad to see me?" This with his face against hers. How could she tell him of the gladness save by stirring a little closer into his arms?

A little draught of remembrance blew into Paradise with a sudden chillness.

"Peter! Oh, Alec, put me down!"

"The worthy husband is dressing, *ma chérie.*" But he put her down on her feet. Then, switching on the lights, he examined her at arm's length.

"*Eh bien,* more beautiful than ever, my Undine! And you love me still?" Half-savagely he swept her into his arms again. "Say so," he commanded.

"I love you, Alec." Her voice was adorable, hardly above a whisper, deep with emotions stirring tumultuously within her, her eyes opened wider looking into his, held with the mesmeric ecstasy of love.

Even as they stood clinging together a step sounded on the stairs and in a flash they were apart, Mona holding a flushed face to the fire, her back to the door, while Alec took a cigarette from his case.

"...and so I arrive, wet and weary, after a journey that was obviously one of the cardinal punishments of purgatory," he was saying as Peter entered.

Mona gave a quick glance at Peter's unperturbed face and hated herself for the deceit, but a moment later she forgot it in the tiny thrill that shot through her as, unobserved, Alec touched her hand.

Dinner was a strange, uncomfortable meal. The conversation seemed to flag until vivified almost nervously by Mona. She could not bear Peter's quiet voice to cease speaking, for when he did it seemed as though there were other voices in the room. Bred from the heavy beating of her heart, they shouted her secret aloud, shouted until Peter must hear, must listen. Alec was composed enough, only his eyes were dark with a strange excitement and Mona felt, rather than noticed that he scarcely ate anything.

"We shall have a new Government ... you remember that fence in the long paddock ... a touch of Arab in him ... will make a magnificent hunter..."

Only snatches of what they were saying reached her as through a shifting fog.

*

Afterwards they sat round the fire, the lights casting soft shadows on the group made them seem the impersonation of quiet contentment. The howling wind and beating rain outside were surely alien to this happy group. Yet Mona, glancing at the faces of the two men, both of whom she loved in different ways, was fearful – to lose the present, to face the future, to regret the past.

'Why is life so complicated?' she asked herself. 'If only Alec had Peter's strength and reliability of character, or Peter...'

She hesitated. What was so attractive about Alec? His virility, his passionate, warm-blooded nature? It sounded horrid in words yet, materialised, was so irresistible.

Peter, rising suddenly, dispersed her reverie.

"I must go out to the stables," he said apologetically. "One of the horses is ill and Jackson is sitting up with him. I said I would have a look at him last thing."

"Take a coat," said Mona. "It's still raining hard."

"I shall be all right, darling," smiled Peter.

"The solicitous wife!" Alec's mocking whisper made Mona blush. Then a moment later, as the door shut, he looked at her almost angrily.

"You drive me mad! I'm so jealous!"

And Mona smiled, delighting in the first realisation of her power to move him. Quite abruptly Alec got up from his chair and stood facing the fire. There was a second's silence. Then he spoke in a quiet, determined way.

"I am going abroad tomorrow."

"Alec!" With a little cry Mona was on her feet beside him, touching his arm with an insistent hand. "It's not true! You can't. Oh, where are you going?"

"I'm going to Jamaica. Undine, darling, are you coming with me?"

Mona stood for a moment incredulous. The whole thing seemed incomprehensible, too gigantic to grasp in a minute. Alec, with his beloved smile and deep voice which thrilled her beyond expression, was going away, away from her, from England, from the environment to which he had seemed indivisibly connected. Then, most astounding of all, he was asking her, his brother's wife, to go with him, to leave everything, to forsake England, her home, her friends, and Peter...

Alec didn't wait for her answer. He put his arms round Mona and drew her close to him.

"Listen, my darling," he said in his deep voice. "We would leave Bristol tomorrow evening on an R.O. boat. Think of the marvellous adventure of starting off into an unknown world, leaving behind all the troubles and worries of the old. The first few days we will have of bad weather will be like the dispelling of our last doubts, as they merge into the southern sunshine. Then we will come to Jamaica, the island of perpetual spring. Deep valleys of wondrous beauty, filled with brilliant flowers and tropical fruits and, towering above them, giant mountains, their slopes covered with dense forests and here and there tiny villages. Above one of them, at a place called Belle Vue, I own a bungalow. You would love it, Undine, built more than a hundred years ago, the veranda running round the house looks right over a great valley to the sea. In the mornings we could watch the yellow sun peeping softly through the mountain mists, rising to the blazing heat of the day, and in the evening…" Alec drew a deep breath and tightened his arm, "…we would see it setting behind the forests of palm trees, deepening at last into the sea like a ball of fire. And then we would feel the cool breezes rise on the wings of the night. Arcadia, Undine, waiting for you and me!"

He stopped speaking, yet Mona's vivid imagination was aflame, seeing the beauty he had painted, putting in the colours, and visualising the fields, crimson, blue and yellow, the orange trees green and gold, the brown naseberries, the Mexican poppies, scarlet and black, the custard apples and mangoes, and from all the subtle perfumes, scenting the air with fragrance, distilling love into the mind, heart and body of the breather, every sense drugged with ecstasy. Arcadia? Or, with Alec, Paradise! Yet how could she answer? And, woman-like, she played for time.

"How could I leave here?" she faltered.

"So easily. I will go to Bristol tomorrow morning and see that a cabin is properly booked and everything as comfortably arranged as possible. I will say goodbye before I leave. Then with just enough time to catch the boat I will return here and wait for you at the end of the park. Your maid, if she can be sworn to secrecy, can go by train with the luggage and meet us at the quay."

"Darling," his voice deepened with passion, "say you'll come. Promise me now."

What could she say, his mouth just touching hers, awaiting an answer, her whole being thrilling like a violin to a master's touch.

"Answer me, Undine, beautiful dream girl. God, how I love you! *Answer me.*"

"Yes." The word was so faint he could hardly hear. For a moment he paused, the indrawing of a deep breath, the adoration of the divine. Then, human with desire, he kissed her again and again, murmuring half-broken sentences into the whiteness of her neck and the softness of her hair.

Only a step outside the window, but Mona heard.

"I can't face Peter. Good night, darling." She disappeared through the darkness of the door and Peter, entering a moment later, found Alec smoking alone before a dying fire.

Upstairs Mona pressed cool hands to her throbbing head. What had she done? She sank down on the low window-seat and tried to think.

Alec or Peter? The eternal triangle, the subject of endless jokes. Yet there was a pathetic lack of humour in the situation when it was personal.

Alec or Peter? It seemed she could never give herself wholly to either. What a hopeless tangle she was making of her life!

And suddenly Mona started to pray with all the intensity of her convent days, and the force of despair.

'Oh God, show me a way out!'

CHAPTER XVI

"Oh, Miss Mona, don't!"

In moments of stress or excitement Annette invariably forgot Mona was married. She stood now against the door, her kind face wrinkled with emotion. Alec had just left after an ostentatious goodbye, with a look for Mona that contradicted his farewell words. It had been an effort to tell Annette about Alec and now the deed was done she avoided the consternation in those straightforward eyes.

With Annette, Mona still felt like the small child liable to be forbidden jam for tea as a punishment for disobedience or put to bed early for more serious offences. There was a pause after Annette's first outburst, then as Mona did not speak, she continued,

"You wouldn't be leaving His Lordship like that, Miss Mona, he who worships the ground you walk on and is worth a million of the other! You're being led away by his dark eyes and tight waist. He ain't got nothing behind that handsome face. Do you think he would stick to you if you was to lose your looks? 'Course he wouldn't. Off like a flash after the next pretty face, while His Lordship ... he'd love you all the more. Oh, Miss Mona dear, you take the advice of an old woman who has loved you all your life since you was a baby. Don't you be led away by fair words. Words is easily forgotten and don't mean much either."

"But I love him, Annette."

Annette's sniff was derisive.

"And supposing he doesn't marry you even after his Lordship gets a divorce?"

Divorce! Somehow Mona hadn't faced the thought of notoriety in the mud of the Divorce Courts. She did not mind social ostracism, but she shrank from the sneers, the publicity. She visualised the glaring headlines,

'MARQUIS DIVORCES HIS WIFE.'

'LOVE FOR HALF-BROTHER.'

She wasn't ignorant or stupid, but she had merely forgotten to face the future, to think what would be the consequence of her actions.

Divorce – misconduct – hard words. They broke against the glamour of love, damaging the gilding of romance.

Romance! The word recalled her honeymoon and a little episode flitted into her thoughts on a tiny wind of remembrance. They had been in Paris, the beloved Paris of Mona's schooldays, and one evening, after a strenuous day of shopping and gaiety, they had returned to the quiet of their hotel overlooking the Tuileries Gardens. The sun was setting in a blaze of red and gold, the sky above a dazzling clear blue. Below in the street the hurrying traffic seemed to laugh with the joy of youth and life, the high noisy horns of the motors like cries of triumphant children at play.

Mona had put out her hand to Peter with a little confiding gesture and he had held it tightly. Both utterly content, they had watched silently.

'If only our life could always be like this,' Mona had thought, and in that instant a resounding report startled her. The peace was shattered. Loud cries and noises echoing upwards from the street. Only two cars colliding, but to her it seemed a bad omen. For a moment she had clung to Peter, then he had laughed at her fright.

"You mustn't be frightened at things, darling," he said. "Nothing can hurt you now, you are my wife."

"Nothing?" questioned Mona – a tiny cloud was still shadowing her happiness.

"Only yourself," answered Peter with deeper insight than he knew.

"Only yourself!" The words rang in her head now – was she deliberately murdering her happiness, or was she grasping it with both hands?

Annette recalled her from her reverie.

"Are you going to take Togs, My Lady?"

It was the perfect lady's maid speaking, her real feelings hidden behind a mask of servitude.

Togs! To be left behind, his faithful eyes pleading to be taken, his little stumpy tail drooping with disappointment. Why, why should things be so difficult? Why should her heart be torn in half?

"Oh, Annette!" The Marchioness was gone. The child cried out in perplexity to the one being who had always soothed her worries, straightened her tangles, and in a moment she was sobbing on the shoulder of the only mother she had ever known.

"There, there, dearie." Annette did not attempt to stem the tide of tears. A woman weeps and washes away much of the agony. Expression eliminates a hurt far sooner than repression.

A quarter of an hour later, having left Annette packing – a scowl on her face and muttering under her breath – Mona walked round the house with the morbid idea of saying goodbye. Only parting from something we know well gives us a perspective of its true value and makes us realise how unconsciously it has grown to be part of ourselves, twining tendrils of affection round our heart.

This was the high hall into which Peter had carried her according to the old country custom on their return from the honeymoon – this, the secret stairway up which they had once fled like naughty children to escape "callers", this, the little bronze figure of a nymph that Peter had bought in Paris because, he said, it was like her. Mona hesitated in front of it. Could she take it away with her? She remembered how they had loved its delicate airy poise, and how one evening she had surprised Peter by dressing up in soft enfolding veils, loosing her long hair, and dancing in the twilight.

"Am I like the statue?" she had asked him, flushed from the exertion, and for an answer Peter had kissed her mouth, her hair and, lastly, her little bare feet.

What was the point of being sentimental about the old life if she was leaving it for the new? She would leave the nymph chained to the home whose bonds she had broken.

She hurried past the door of Peter's study – she couldn't face the room that was such an embodiment of his tastes and interests, the gun-cases in the corner, the fox's mask and brush, souvenirs of his 'blooding' at a very tender age, the hooves of his favourite horses made into ink-pots and paper weights, memorials of a man's best friends.

The desk at which he always wrote, littered with papers, books and pipes, and, above the *mêlée* a large portrait of herself, smiling with the happiness of a week-old bride, the pictured eyes looking at Peter as he wrote.

She remembered her first introduction to the room.

"This is my sanctum," Peter had announced gaily. "'Tis here I grapple with the affairs of my kingdom."

"How important! "Mona had teased. "And no one must disturb His Majesty. I suppose even I am barred without?"

"Never!" Peter had answered. "Because you couldn't disturb me if you tried!" And he had picked her up and dropped her into one of the two big leather armchairs drawn near the fire.

"Your throne, O Queen! From henceforth I share the joys and sorrows of my kingdom."

"Only the joys," she had cried laughingly. Then, suddenly serious, she had thrown her arms round Peter's neck and drawn his head down to hers. "And the sorrows, Peter darling," she had whispered.

How carelessly we promise and then find fulfilment too difficult a task, our words but dust before the wind of circumstance!

Her own writing-table in the wide window of the morning-room, bought especially for her because Peter liked the ornamentation of fat cupids staggering under the weight of huge bunches of grapes. On the top were three photographs, Sally radiant in court dress, feathers on her head, a bouquet in her hands, Peter, an enlarged snapshot – he would never be photographed properly – Peter with his look of serious preoccupation as he tried to make his mount, a thoroughbred chestnut mare, face the camera, and lastly Togs, frightfully intense and intelligent, his ears pricked as someone had said "Rats!"

Mona picked them up almost defiantly, then paused as though to replace them.

'Don't go,' said her conscience.

'Don't go,' cried the trees in the garden outside. 'Think how you will miss us in the spring!'

"Don't go," said Sally in her silver frame.

"Don't go," said the real Togs, following her around and sensing with the sharpened intuition of animals that something was wrong.

Only Peter's photograph seemed to say nothing. Instead she felt as though his whole house were vibrant with his personality, that it held her a prisoner. Escape was really impossible, a fantastic dream.

A picture of Alec, painted years ago but still incredibly like him, laughed at her from the wall.

"I have but to beckon," it said, "then see if these can hold you!"

With a crash of breaking glass Mona dropped the three photographs she held on to the floor and, with a little cry expressing an agony beyond tears, she ran from the room.

Yet fervent prayers are generally answered and Mona's decision was made for her by a Higher Power. Alec waited in vain at the end of the park till at last, cursing and blaspheming, he realised his defeat, while Mona, travelling swiftly towards Scotland with Peter, found her feelings too chaotic for coherent thought.

The Duke of Glenac had died that morning.

CHAPTER XVII

The new Duchess of Glenac was half-hidden in a deep armchair drawn in front of the great fireplace, where a log fire smouldered and smoked, refusing to give any heat and assuage the cold of the high Scottish hall. Her sombre garments merged into the deepening shadows until only her white face and hands were as ghostly wraiths, eerily inanimate because she was so still. The pale cheeks and dark lines under the pensive eyes were not entirely an illusion of the twilight. The last few days in this house of death had been a physical strain. The funeral was over and the numerous relatives had departed, some of them the quaint persons who appear at the announcement of a death in the family, coming apparently from unknown burrows to claim kinship with the corpse, then returning to the oblivion from whence they came.

Mona had played the part of hostess to perfection, had housed, fed and entertained the strange dour Scottish cousins, the flighty excited-about-the-will relations from the south and mysterious executors, trustees, and solicitors who were overwhelmingly full of self-importance and sanctimonious grief.

Mona had loved the late Duke, although their acquaintance had been a short one. A grand old man of a grand old family. And when she gazed at his peaceful face, from which many years had dropped – wiped away by the kind hand of Death – she thanked God that he had never been hurt by any scandal of hers.

"And you never shall be!" she whispered, tears in her eyes. "For your sake I will honour the name I inherit from you. Only help me!"

He had been a stern martinet to himself as well as to others, esteeming 'family pride' a virtue, making it for himself the keynote of his life. A terrible blow had been dealt him by the behaviour of his second wife, but no word of complaint ever passed his lips. He had only withdrawn more and more into the seclusion of his cold northern home.

The surrounding mountains with their gaunt rugged tops and isolated sides resembled, perhaps, his indomitable pride and reticence, the stern code of the Victorian era that refused to be swayed or influenced by modern thought.

Many people had loved him, but their affection held a deep reverence. Mona had been amazed at the genuine grief of many of the mourners – old gillies, ancient retainers and pensioners, many of whom walked forty miles to the funeral. Listening to their talk of bygone days, she learned many lessons and realised with a sense of awe the responsibility of the empty throne. Peter and she were to 'carry on'. This tiny kingdom must not lack a king, a king its subjects would respect.

The wind whistled down the chimney and a sudden gust caused the windows to rattle. Somewhere in the house a door slammed with a startling bang. Mona shivered and sank further into the chair. At this moment Alec was perhaps on deck, basking in the tropic sunlight. The great boat would be moving slowly on the smooth waters, the attendants white-garbed and attentive to every physical want, while the wonderful sunsets, the glorious climate and seductive atmosphere were a combination leading irresistibly to mental wellbeing. Resolutely Mona dismissed the thought. The past was finished – a chapter closed, which in time, she prayed, would be obliterated.

Already the spell of his personality was beginning to wane. The compelling power of his attraction lay only in his mesmeric bodily magnetism. There were no depths in Alec to make the heart grow fonder in absence. Irresistible as he had been to Mona, his image was fading. She had no regrets now, only a calm acceptance of the fate that had turned her from him even at the eleventh hour. Soon she knew he would become merely a shadowy memory, a milestone, it maybe, in her life, standing not at crossroads, but on the broad highway, marking the continuance of her journey with Peter.

Togs's shrill welcoming bark disturbed her thoughts and a moment later she heard Peter's voice. He had returned from speeding the last of the departing guests, driving them over miles of moorland to the tiny wayside station to catch the evening express to London.

"Hello, darling," he greeted his wife. "Why are you all in the dark? "He rang for the lamps as he spoke. "We must have electric light put into this place."

"Have you had tea, Peter?" Mona asked.

"Yes, thanks, I called at the parson's on my way home. Priceless old man, terribly Scottish and Presbyterian. You'll hate the church, darling – exactly like a whitewashed barn."

"It's your living, isn't it, Peter – can't we turn him out?"

"Not very well." Peter hesitated – here was a difficult explanation. "Of course, darling, an exchange might be arranged, but you see all the people round here like that sort of service. Anything else they consider popery, and it would be very unpopular. You like the church at Taylsea, dear –

don't you think we had better leave this one alone and let the people go on worshipping in the way they have done for generations?"

He spoke anxiously. In these days it was hard enough to keep peace on a big estate without holding a lighted match to the combustible gas of religious principle, origin of contention through all the ages. But he also knew Mona's strong convictions, convent bred and still narrow-visioned by youth and inexperience.

"I expect you know best, Peter," Mona said sweetly and unexpectedly.

Peter heaved a sigh of relief. He did not know that a little twinge of conscience made her ready to agree with him had the suggestion been to destroy *Notre-Dame*.

A footman brought in the lights and the papers. He also drew the heavy velvet curtains. Mona was glad. The gloom outside depressed her. The dead leaves, blown relentlessly around by the swirling gale, were like lost souls. The damp mist, which veiled the moors and valleys, seemed to be closing round the castle like an advancing evil. But inside the lamps cast warm yellow patches. The fire drew the damp from Peter's boots and absent-mindedly Mona watched it rise.

"By the way, I called for the second post," said Peter. "They only deliver once a day here. One letter for you." He tossed it across to her.

It was from Sally, a short incoherent scrawl, describing hectic gaieties.

Peter opened the papers.

"By Jove!" he exclaimed suddenly, "I see there has been a collision between an R.O. liner and a coal ship – forty lives lost."

"Alec!" Mona rose to her feet with a stifled cry. "Is he hurt? Look quickly..." She rushed to Peter's side and shook his arm agitatedly. Her fear of death for someone she knew was childishly hysterical, but to Peter it held a deeper significance. The white face and the startled dark eyes!

"Why does it matter so terribly?" Peter's question rang out like a pistol-shot but Mona hardly listened. She was devouring the paper with her eyes. Why didn't she answer? This strange trembling creature he hardly recognised as his wife.

"The Eldorado," she said at last in a voice of happy relief. "Alec was on the Karimato."

Peter suddenly put heavy hands on her shoulders and turned her round to face him. The look on his face gave her a shock. Very pale, his mouth was drawn into a tight line that accentuated the determination of a heavy jaw. His grey eyes were like steel – cold and merciless. It was as though she looked into the face of a stranger.

"Answer me!" he said. "How do you know he was? And why does it matter to you?"

"I don't know," Mona faltered, frightened by this strange Peter.

"Are you in love with him?"

"I ... Oh, Peter, don't look at me like that," she pleaded.

"Answer me!"

What was she to say? She did not know herself.

After a moment's silence, Peter, as though answered, asked another question.

"Is Alec in love with you?"

"I suppose so," Mona said miserably, feeling the strength ebbing from her under this terrible cross-examination.

Light seemed to break into Peter's consciousness and make his suspicions a certainty. He remembered going to Mona's bedroom with the telegram that told of his father's death. The startled look on her face as he had opened the door materialised in his memory. She had heard his news in silence.

"We must start for Scotland tonight," he had said at last.

"Tonight!"

He remembered now her odd intonation of the commonplace word. At the time he had been too worried to remark consciously upon it. He had a vague picture of Annette kneeling in front of an open box. Why had she been packing?

"You were going away together." He half-questioned, half-accused.

It was no use pretending any more. Mona found that she couldn't lie to Peter. She wanted to explain to him, but there was no explanation. She craved the protective kindness of the husband who had always calmed her fears. But here in his place was a stern judge, a man with fierce angry eyes and hard gripping hands that hurt. She nodded miserably in answer to his question. This could not be true. It was a dream from which she would awake sobbing. She noticed a small tear in the shoulder of his tweed coat and wondered how he did it.

"My God!" The words seemed jerked from him.

Then the storm broke and Mona shrank before it.

"Alec has always taken everything from me in my life and now he has taken my wife. To think I worshipped you and was almost afraid to touch the elusiveness of you, thinking it innocence. *God!*"

His voice broke for a moment on the bitterly cynical note.

"Peter, *Peter!*" Mona pleaded for mercy, tears blinding her eyes. She must tell him it was untrue. She couldn't remember. What had happened in the past? If only this terrible voice would stop and she could think!

"It's my fault," the deep voice went on. "I should have treated you as human, claimed you as my own, taught you the meaning of passion when you fled from it into my arms. Instead you have other instructors, while I, poor blind fool, believed you immortal. *Immortal!* I know Alec's methods."

Then with a sound of agony breaking into an audible expression, more pitiable than words, Peter seized Mona in his arms, gripping her until she felt her bones must break, until she lay helpless, her head against his shoulder, feeling the roughness of his coat against her cheek, the faint scent of heather and tobacco in her nostrils. Bending his head, Peter looked for a moment at the pale face. The dark eyes were raised to his in frightened supplication, the lashes wet with tears. She looked so innocent, hardly more than a child. The black dress with its white collar made her appear so slim that, at various times in the last few days, Peter had laughed at himself for thinking she might disappear entirely – vanish into the mythical land, the 'Hollow Hills' in which she believed so firmly. For a second Peter weakened. Then a thought of Alec's handsome mocking face made him almost lose control of himself. With a laugh that held no humour he bent his head and kissed her, roughly and passionately, until the room swam around her and her mouth was bruised and hurt. Yet even in that moment of fear, misery and pain, much as she was reluctant to admit it, something within her rejoiced at his primitiveness, the age-old emotion of womanhood swaying before physical superiority, loving a man for his strength.

Almost before she could realise what was happening, Peter, with an oath which made her shudder, threw her from him. She staggered against the sofa, steadying herself with groping fingers. Without another word Peter walked out of the room. The door slammed with a dismal finality.

It was a dream. He would come back. Mona fought with the dizziness sweeping over her. But it was useless. With a desperate feeling of loss she dropped to the floor – and lay quite still.

CHAPTER XVIII

The frightened cry Mona uttered, even the slamming of the oak door, hardly reached Peter's consciousness. There was a sound in his ears that came from within himself and deafened him. Voices, mocking, jeering, accusing, and again weeping for his hurt. He could not think – they prevented him. It was as though a hundred jazz bands played around him, each executing a different tune. He longed for peace – he was in the grip of emotions so alien to his nature that he almost shrank from himself, yet they ran through his being like a weirdly intoxicating fire – revenge, reprisal, vengeance. Then, as if something snapped and an agony beyond tears cried,

"Oh, my dear! *My dear!*"

If he could only kill – the voices seemed to rise in a crescendo of fury. Like an infuriated bull he faced the world – impotent, powerless, alone.

"Mona!" He cried her name aloud. Then with the searing certainty of slow torture, pictures of her passed in his mind. Before they married – her sweet serious eyes raised to his as he talked of lands he had visited, describing journeys and pilgrimages to strange places. Words are inadequate mediums and Peter could never command their service, but Mona endowed them with her vivid imagination, and they became to her as real as if she had seen them.

He had promised to take her to China, the fount of intellectual beauty, to Egypt, whose beauty and atmosphere sway the senses, to California, whose raw loveliness is that of untouched nature, the call of the wild. Her eyes – they had told so much, concealed so much – windows of the soul, revealing unstirred depths – depths of which even she was unaware. Their wedding day – frightened womanhood clouding those virgin eyes. Virginity! It had encircled Mona like a protecting cloud – an atmosphere of reserve – purity. What could describe that inexplicable something that is a state of the soul, not the body?

Mona – aloof, fey, *divine!* Then on an instant a clinging, loving woman, demanding his attention, his love, his desires.

Days of companionship, nights of intimacy! Suddenly Peter's brain became clear, his emotions cold, unobtrusive, as if he were a machine, not a man. He began to think of Alec. The blind rage that had filled him just now was forgotten – it was a judge who looked back to the past and remembered – not a husband. A judge who was to pass judgment. Alec, who had laughed at his reticence, mocked his control, and had plucked the coveted fruit. He, Peter, had waited for the door to open unto him, Alec had picked the lock and for his presumption had been rewarded.

The handsome, debonair face, the lithe, graceful figure, the compelling eyes, the mesmeric voice. Was Mona to blame? She was so young – youth imprisoned in a land of staid grown-ups. She had been hypnotised, drugged by fair words – words that flattered and ensnared her with their golden promises. Vanity, childlike, but still vanity, attribute of eternal *femina*, luring her like an evil will-o'-the-wisp into dangerous bogs. Peter could understand a little the temptation that dazzled her, understand, in spite of a tearing pain in his heart, a wound that was a physical agony as well as a mental one. But he was divided within himself – he was two men. One pleaded for Mona, a counsel for her defence. The other, coldly, dispassionately, summed up the evidence against her. Alec's first visit to Taylsea – they had met before – his obvious delight at the reunion – the pleasure they had shown even then in each other's company. They had played together like children, laughed, talked nonsense, bathed, played tennis, yes – that was all. But Mona had been strange when he left, preoccupied in her thoughts, almost worried. Why?

Mona's journey to London. Why had she returned so unexpectedly? Admittedly she had seen Alec. Had that anything to do with it? It had been as if she ran home to security. What was she running away from? She had clung to Peter as if by physical contact she could bind herself whole-heartedly for eternity. Had conscience or fear of the consequences frightened her? Then Alec's letter had arrived, inviting himself to stay. Mona had been glad. Peter remembered now – a sudden lighting up of her face, a flash of happiness in her eyes, that no acting, however perfect, can assume or hide. She had sung that day, laughed, romped with Togs. In the late afternoon, however, she had been distrait and thoughtful. Sitting alone in the dusk, he had surprised her with tears in her eyes.

"You are not unhappy, darling?" he had asked.

"What is happiness?" she had answered strangely. "If it is to be athrill with life, I am happy. If it is to feel, to love, to learn, I desire it. If it is contentment…"

"But you are content, darling?" he had said, puzzled by this mood.

"Contentment is the wet-nurse of the very young and the reward of the very old," Mona said. "We are not allowed to stagnate in unstirred pools, Peter, we have got to battle with waves and storms – to battle..." Her voice had broken and she had hidden her face in his shoulder. "Peter, there are so many years before us. I do love you – *I do.*" She had said the last words vehemently as if she wished to convince herself. He remembered the intonation now, while at the time he had merely allowed himself to forget the earlier words in the happiness of that profession of love. She so seldom spoke of her love for him, although she demanded articulate verification of his. So she had tried to fight against her desire for Alec! Then he had arrived. Dinner! Mona silent, her cheeks flushed, her eyes slightly dilated. Peter had wondered at the time if she had a touch of fever – afterwards he had forgotten to mention it. He had thought Alec noticed it too, because once he saw watching Mona, a strange expression on his dark face. *God!* How blind he had been!

He had left them alone when he went to see the horses.

As he entered the hall, he thought he saw Mona running up the stairs. He had called her, but she had not answered, and Alec had said she been gone some time. She had avoided him – not wishing to say goodnight. Why? And later, she had been asleep or pretending, and her door locked!

Alec had left the next morning, his destination Cornwall, he had said. The farewells had been quite natural. Peter had merely been glad to see him go as he wanted Mona to himself. She had been strange that day – refusing to motor with him in the afternoon in spite of a promise to accompany him to Cheddar, where he had an appointment. At lunch she had talked feverishly, as if she was afraid of silence – jumping from one subject to another, laughing heartily yet eating nothing in spite of his efforts to tempt her appetite. When he left, she had kissed him goodbye and for a moment he had thought she was going to tell him something.

"You were going to say...?" he had prompted her.

Her face had been very white, almost strained.

"Nothing. There is nothing to say. Goodbye, darling."

It had been a long day, cold and windy up on the hills. He had looked forward to his return home and a quiet evening with Mona. *Mona* – she was all his life – he asked nothing else. He hurried his appointment and a good hour before he had expected to be free, he was speeding homewards.

A telegram awaited him. Carelessly he tore it open, then stiffened to startled attention. His father was dead. Before even thoughts of sorrow and loss must come practical arrangements – he must reach Glenac by tomorrow morning. Hastily he gave orders for the car, the packing of luggage, the notifying of relations by telegram and telephone.

"Where is Her Ladyship?"

"Upstairs, in her room, My Lord."

Mona would be sorry, because she loved the Duke. She would want to be at his funeral. He knocked hastily at her door and entered. Anette had been kneeling on the floor in front of a large box. Mona was standing by her. She raised her startled eyes to his.

"I..." then she had stopped.

"My father died this morning," Peter said quietly. "We must go up to Glenac tonight. Will that be all right?"

"Tonight?" Why had her voice seemed so strange?

"Yes, dear."

"Oh, it's ... I'm..." and Mona had broken down, half crying, half fainting. Peter had picked her up in his arms and put her on the bed.

"Leave her to me, My Lord, it's the shock." Annette had whisked him out of the room, but was worried as he had had no idea Mona would be so upset.

Then there had been so much to see to that he had forgotten. Why had she been packing? That night, by her own confession, she knew Alec was sailing on the Karimato, the R.O. line to Jamaica – Alec's bungalow! God! Peter knew of two women who had spent illicit 'honeymoons' in that picturesque fools' paradise, imagining it evergreen until Alec had tired of them. Mona, *his Mona*, would have shared their fate and awoken one morning to have found the despoiler was tired of his spoils! Sanity would rend the veil of illusion, and the aftermath of passion would show them romance as a cancerous growth. They would return shame-faced to the world they had so easily renounced and try to clamber back onto the pedestals of respectability. One of them had come to Peter for help. She had lost everything – position, husband, children, friends. How he had pitied her and admired the brave effort she was making to reconstruct a ruined life.

"The pity of it!" he had said.

"The flesh indeed is weak," she had answered.

Oh, Mona, *Mona*, that unclean hands should have touched you, and you should have thought them clean.

Alec had held her in his arms, had loved her as Peter had never dared. The time in London – he must have frightened her a little – no, it had been conscience. How they must have laughed at the husband who stayed at home while his wife went to her lover. Why had her door been locked to him the night before Alec left? If Mona was asleep Peter never disturbed her, but she had never locked him out. And then they were going away together.

The evidence was at an end. There was a breathing silence, as when a powerful voice ceases to speak. And now must come the verdict. Mercy had pleaded for pity. Justice had shown the truth.

"Guilty!" The word seemed to be spoken aloud, then Peter realised he had said it himself. *Guilty!*

His hands were wet – he was lying on the grass. How long he had been there he did not know. All round was the damp darkness and a thick mist was enveloping the night. It was freezingly cold, the wind had dropped. Peter staggered to his feet. He was soaked to the skin and exhausted as if he had been fighting. He was dead-beat. Without mental effort, almost unconsciously, he took his bearings. He was about a mile from the house, although how he had got there he had no idea. He recognised the tree under which he had lying – it had been his hiding-place as a child. His footsteps had led him to an old haunt. Somehow, the idea vaguely comforted him. The confessional of many sorrows had now received this greatest of all. Majestic, the old oak towered above him – remaining upright under the swirling elements of a century – an example. His life must be like that – impervious to storms however violent. He must not weaken.

"If thine eye offend thee, pluck it out."

Mona ... *Mona...*

The house was very still. At the passage which led to Mona's room Peter paused. She was there, dark hair shading the deep eyes, white body thinly veiled. Alec ... Mona ...

God! Could he ever look on that beautiful face again without shuddering, without thinking of them together?

"If thine eye offend thee…"

The house was very still. Perhaps happiness lay dying, Peter sat writing far into the night. Outside great oaks raised their branches defiantly to the lowering heavens.

CHAPTER XIX

Would the night ever end? Mona tossed side to side of her bed, restless in body and mind. The situation became as a mighty forest, hemming her in on every side. She had lost her way – the more she puzzled the more desperate became her plight. Explanations are invariably unconvincing. Our feelings are too vast, too complicated for description. We start so bravely. "I felt strangely stirred ..." and there we are defeated. "It was like…" nothing tangible, nothing we can translate into commonplace sensations or write for our friends to read and understand. Even a carefully considered action may yet be but an impulse of a hitherto unknown part of our nature, the contradictions, the variations, the diversity of our moods, all comprising one character, one personality, which is unaware of itself.

Knowledge is a strange, tricky subject that few people master. Women boast of their comprehension of men, but the only people they deceive by their pretensions are themselves. The Peter who had thrown her roughly from him, whose face, twisted in anger, was strange and awe-inspiring, could not be the husband whose gentle loving kindness had been a shelter from the world. She had imagined that every thought behind those grave eyes was familiar to her. But now it was a stranger to whom she must explain her actions. A stranger – from whose mercy she must crave forgiveness. Had she ever known him she wondered.

At last a faint light began to glimmer through the curtains and, as so often happens after 'a white night', the day brought the desired solace of sleep. Mona, worn out, dropped into a dreamless slumber, awakening to find the clock striking ten and Annette bringing in her breakfast.

"His Grace left early this morning," she announced. "He gave me this note for you, My-La... Your Grace."

She watched Mona anxiously as she opened the black-edged envelope. Annette, as she expressed it herself, "had a nose for trouble", and she sensed it now.

The paper rustled in nervous fingers and for a moment the writing danced before Mona's eyes. Then she read,

'Dear Mona,

I gather you do not now intend an open breach, and I sincerely hope my supposition is correct, for the sake of the family. In this case I feel you will prefer to make your home in London. The lease of 62 South Street, Park Lane – a house on my estate – has fallen in. I am instructing my solicitors to make it over to you by deed of gift. However, please consider that Taylsea is also at your disposal. On the rare occasions when I am present, I will use the west wing, so our arrangements will in no way interfere with one another. If there is anything you want, please do not hesitate to let me know.

Peter.'

She could not grasp the full significance until she had read it again. It was incredible, impossible! Peter meant them to live apart. She must implore him, beg him to come back, tell him he was wrong, that her affair with Alec was not a guilty love, only a flirtation, an infatuation, which was over now, finally and forever. She was innocent, and he must know. Then pride rose, a red burning flame from the ashes of unhappiness. He chose to leave callously without saying goodbye, to cast her away as unclean, to consider her innocence tainted. He should beg forgiveness and plead with her before she pardoned him.

'Perhaps he will not desire to be reinstated,' whispered a fearful heart, but pride closed her ears.

'I don't care,' she told herself. And tried to believe it.

Presently, while Annette was packing, Mona commenced to write an answer to Peter's note.

'Dear Peter,' she started, then sat for ages thinking in vain. It was so different. Odd how she had never written to Peter before, for they had never been apart. She would miss him, came a tiny aching thought, miss the cheery companionship, the joy of intellectual discourse in the car, and the more intimate happiness of knowing one is loved selflessly and devotedly.

'Can I see you?' she wrote. Then a memory of the anger in Peter's eyes last night made her tear it up. How dare he imply with his bitter, scathing voice that she was degraded! His roughness had hurt her, yet a colour flamed in her cheeks at the remembrance of the passion in his kisses. Then she questioned herself almost furiously. Was she to be swayed and captivated by every man who appealed to her body with the primitive seduction of strength? Where was the fastidiousness of her girlhood? Then she fled from crude nature, horrified and disgusted. Was she wanton or merely natural? Was the cultivation of intellect convention and the finesse of civilisation to be absolutely as nothing beside the first call of the senses? Polish destroyed and demolished by heat?

She would not write to Peter. She would go to London. She would view life on a wider field. Her own tiny garden had grown weeds where she had planted flowers. The roses blossomed out of reach, stalwart oaks had blown down in the wind and become but dead wood. It had grown into a wilderness beyond her care and comprehension.

"We will go to London, Annette," she announced.

"Yes, Miss ... I mean Your Grace! I never can remember," Annette answered, her arms full of silk and lace, wonderful confections over which she had spent many hours in the last few days in embroidering ducal coronets. Mona had laughed at her for a snob, but Annette had persisted.

"Wear all you are entitled to, Miss Mona," she said earnestly. "As my mother always says, 'Render under Caesar the things which are Caesar's instead of worrying about the things as ain't.'"

"Annette," said Mona suddenly, "I have an idea! We will motor down. It will be too lovely and we can stay at York on the way. I shall take the Rolls and drive it myself."

"Now, Miss Mona, don't you do anything of the sort," said Annette in horror. "His Grace wouldn't like it."

"Who cares?" said Mona recklessly and, leaving Annette still protesting, she ran downstairs.

Poor Annette. She had experienced Mona's driving before and had been frightened almost into hysterics. Mona slipped out of a side door and walked through the yards to the back drive that led to the stables and garage.

The stable boys and grooms saluted respectfully. They greatly admired the new Duchess.

"A damn sight better than the last," as one old retainer expressed it.

She found Ackman, the chauffeur, in the garage.

"I'm going to drive the car down to London, Ackman. Will you have it round about twelve o'clock?"

Ackman hesitated uneasily.

"His Grace said it was to stay up here, as your Grace would use the other car at Taylsea."

Had Peter arranged the whole universe in a few hours? Mapping out her life without consulting her? Was she at every turn to find His Grace's arrangements barring the way, perverting her plans? If he chose to go his own way she would go hers, regardless of any schemes save her own.

"You can go down by train tomorrow and bring the car back, Ackman. I will take it down today."

"Yes, your Grace."

A victory, even if a tiny one. Then the elation passed and Mona sighed. It was going to be awfully lonely doing things by herself.

An hour later the car stood at the door and Mona took the wheel. Annette, with disapproval written all over her face, climbed in behind. Mona wouldn't let her sit in front because Annette's hysterical "Oh, Miss Mona!" and clutchings at the side of the car made her nervous.

The first forty miles were over moorland. High mountains, snow-capped, towered above them and the road ran like a ribbon along the slopes, sometimes rising until it entered the low clouds and they were enveloped in a thick grey mist, which made driving a difficult task. It was intensely cold and freezing hard. But Mona, wrapped in warm furs, enjoyed every second of the journey. Later a storm broke over them, but luckily the car was well covered in, and they did not suffer.

At lunchtime they picnicked by the roadside. A thermos flask provided them with hot coffee, and the butler had been wise enough to pack a small bottle of cherry brandy, a glass of which revived their spirits and kept out the cold. However, they could not linger long. Already they were behind time. The bad weather had impeded their progress. They started off again, but the right roads were more difficult to determine than Mona had imagined. In this desolate part of the country there were no signposts. And many misleading by-paths were not marked on the road maps. About five o'clock they drew up at a wayside inn for tea. Twilight was falling, but they had still a great many miles to cover before they could find shelter for the night. Mona had given up any idea of York and searched a guide for nearer towns that could boast of a decent hotel. The landlady informed them that they had side-tracked from the London road, which meant that they must retrace their steps for about five miles. But the news did not spoil their enjoyment of tea, hot scones and newly-baked bread.

It was almost dark when they started again and the road was very slippery. They had driven about twenty miles when, rounding a corner, the car skidded. Before Mona had time to realise what had happened, they were off the narrow road, and the next moment they were firmly imbedded in the deep wayside ditch.

"Well, this is pleasant," she said mournfully as the car refused to move an inch and Annette, after a first shrill scream, had become inarticulate.

The surrounding country looked bare and desolate – there were no lights to tell of human habitation and the road was deserted.

"It seems we shall have to stay the night here," said Mona, "and I'm so cold."

For about a quarter of an hour she sat listening to Annette's murmurings of 'a judgment' and mournful prophecies of their both dying of the cold. It was freezing hard. Already tiny icicles were forming on the windscreen. Mona, drawing her furs round her, wondered where Peter was. Would he be worried if he knew of his wife's plight?

She might have killed herself. Perhaps then he would have regretted his unkindness. She imagined the headlines of the newspaper,

'DUCHESS FOUND DEAD IN A DITCH'

'TERRIBLE ACCIDENT IN THE HIGHLANDS'

Supposing he didn't care? He might even be relieved. It would leave him free – free to marry again. As though stung to action by the thought, Mona blew the horn again and again in the hope of attracting some stray passer-by. Suddenly down the road she saw lights approach. It was evidently a high dog-cart, being driven rapidly. She sprang out of the car and stood in the middle of the road, waving and shouting.

"What's the matter? "A man spoke, an educated voice with just the suspicion of a Scottish burr.

"I've skidded into the ditch," Mona answered, pointing at the car. "Can you get someone to pull me out?"

The stranger climbed slowly out of the cart – a tall man and quite young, Mona judged. He looked at the car and shook his head.

"You'll have to leave it till the morning. In the meantime," he hesitated, "you'd better come home with me. It's better than staying here."

"Oh, Miss Mona, if we stay here we shall be frozen to death."

The stranger started. He had been unaware of Annette's presence.

"It's only my maid," Mona smiled. "She has been terrifying me with gloomy predictions."

"Do you mind getting into my gig? "he asked. "I live about a mile down the road."

Mona climbed on to the high seat and assisted Annette, while the stranger put Mona's dressing-case in the back.

"The luggage will be all right till the morning," he reassured them. "There are no thieves in Lanackgreigg."

He took the reins and with a "Gee-up, Dobbin," they started off into the darkness.

CHAPTER XX

The stranger's domain was a small cottage built under the lee of a hill and surrounded by trees. An elderly woman opened the door and stared at the new-comers somewhat suspiciously.

"My housekeeper," introduced the stranger. "Jean, these ladies have had a motor accident and are going to stay the night with us."

"Come awa' ben," Jean invited smilingly, and led them into a small sitting room, obviously a man's room, but comfortable and cheerful, with a large fire and a table laid for supper.

After they had warmed themselves for a few minutes Mona went upstairs with Jean and was shown the guest room. An enormous double bed covered with a patchwork quilt, filled most of the available space and the only decorations were three illuminated texts. But Jean regarded it with much pride.

"Ye, it's an awfu' fine room," she said, "an' ye ken the Master's mither deid here two years sine."

Mona slipped off her hat and coat, powdered her nose and went downstairs. The stranger was waiting on supper for her, and the delicious aroma coming from a large stew-pot made Mona hungrier than ever.

The sitting room, or rather living room, for, with the adjoining kitchen, the ground-floor was complete, was an odd mixture of good taste and early-Victorian monstrosities. The furniture was mostly plain oak, dark with age, the craft of many a bygone generation. The pictures were few, but original prints, in all probability worth several hundreds of pounds apiece. A glass cabinet contained a dinner service of early Worcester and a specimen bowl of Rockingham blue. But the ornaments on the mantelpiece were the highly coloured products of German manufacture.

An upright cottage piano was ornamented with a brocade cover, from which hung innumerable small tassels, and was crowned by a glass case containing a dozen stuffed hummingbirds. A huge bookcase stretching to the ceiling covered one side of the room. The bright covers of the books – red, green and blue – gave a note of colour to the sombre walls, which were covered with a dark paper, faded and discoloured by damp. Even a quick glance showed Mona that the latest modern novels held their place among more serious literary works, and medical journals. Wells, Galsworthy, Gilbert Frankau, Robert Hichens, Michael Arlen rubbed shoulders with Saint-Simon, Turgeniev, Balzac and Voltaire.

They sat down at the table and Mona regarded her companion curiously. He was a tall man with red hair just greying at the temples. His face was weather-beaten and tanned, his clothes shabby and ill-fitting. Yet withal he looked a gentleman and spoke like one.

"It was lucky I chose tonight to visit my nearest neighbour, who lives five miles away," he remarked. "I say 'chose' but that is hardly correct or true, for I am a doctor, one of those unlucky men to whom they say, 'Come, and he cometh' whatever the hour of the day or night."

"I should think you find it terribly lonely here," Mona answered, "unless your practice is a very large one."

"A very scattered one," he replied. "My nearest patient, as I told you, is five miles away and my farthest about forty."

"By the way," he added, smiling, "my name is Faulkner – David Faulkner."

"And mine is…" said Mona, she hesitated a moment, "Mona Gordon."

"I'm admiring your library," said Mona presently.

"Because you are surprised to meet Mr. McKenna and Mr. Arlen in the wilds! Oh yes," he smiled as Mona protested, all the more vehemently because his supposition was correct, "it's unusual, I grant you, but my apology for upsetting your theories on the Scotsman's literature is that I write a little myself."

"How clever of you!" Mona was genuinely interested. "Under your own name?"

"No, my *nom de plume* is Sandy MacWeasel. You won't have heard of me," he added modestly. "My circulation is only north of the Tweed."

Sandy MacWeasel! Of course Mona had heard of him, the Scottish W. W. Jacobs, whose dry humour made his countrymen regard his works as household gods. Peter had laughed heartily over his last story, *Ye ken Robin?* But Mona had found the dialect as difficult to understand as a foreign language.

She told him so now and he made her a mock apology. But when she questioned him further, he was as bashful about his books as a schoolboy with his first prize.

"Writing a book seems to me on a parallel with child-bearing," he said at last. "Firstly, it is conceived, then with labour brought into the world, nourished and developed until sent to the publishers as to a school, moulded and disciplined into shape until the finished product makes a *début* with all the uncertain shyness of an *ingenue.* A critical world receives it indifferently. Few *débutantes* make a stir socially or literarily. But the fortunates are given a place in the hearts of the great public."

Supper over, they drew chairs up in front of the fire and Dr. Faulkner, after first asking Mona's permission, lit his pipe.

"Yes," he said meditatively, "this is a very desolate part of the country, but loneliness teaches many lessons one has no time to learn in the midst of civilisation."

"I am going to London now to escape solitude," said Mona.

"Perhaps you are flying from yourself," he answered, "trying to chloroform your own thoughts."

"I think I am," Mona said simply.

"Then don't, lassie. If a patient of mine has an evil growth inside him I don't appease his pain with drugs, letting it grow larger in secret and doping him into a belief in its non-existence. No – I cut it out – and the agony of the moment is worth the after-relief. Face it, lassie, and afterwards you'll thank God for His mercy in giving you the strength."

"Do you believe in God's mercy?" asked Mona. She did not know why she asked the question, but this earnest Scotsman seemed to have a vast experience of life which his solitary existence could hardly account for.

"I do," he answered. "I've seen Him part a married couple by death, when for one to lose the other was like amputating a limb. I've seen Him smite down the first-born or let the good folk starve in the gutter while the evil flourish on ill-gotten gains. But underneath it all runs a merciful far-seeing objective that we, with our finite minds, find incomprehensible to grasp."

Suddenly Mona felt she must ask his advice on her own problems. She had concealed her identity, but she must tell her troubles to someone or go mad.

"Supposing a girl was in love with a man," she began, "and made up her mind to go away with him, and then something unforeseen prevented the elopement so that she went back to her husband. And after a few days she realised that her love for the other man had been only a madness, a mirage, and she was sorry. Yet accidentally her husband, who was the kindest person in the world, found out and left her in anger and arranged that in future their paths were to separate. So she lost everything. Would you call that the mercy of God?" Mona had no idea of the bitterness in her voice.

"And don't you think you deserve punishment?" asked David. And neither of them noticed that the discussion had become personal.

"You vowed the solemn oaths on your wedding-day, to love, honour and obey. At the first temptation you decide to break them and yield to the impulse to gratify your desires. Do you not know that you have a greater work in the world than merely questioning your emotions? Why should you, one mere scrap of humanity, be allowed to upset the pattern of the universe? Some of the greatest pleasures come to mankind in pursuit of duty – duty to God, duty to one's neighbour. You live in a society that fills lazy hours by 'being in love' with so-and-so – any Tom, Dick, or Harry, until a better quarry appears. Take a thought, instead, of the millions of women who stick to their men through thick and thin, working for them until bedridden with age, too busy to question their devotion or psycho-analyse their feelings. If duty were the principal lesson in the education of children, the world would be a far better place today. To every wife who told me she was 'in love' with another man I would say, 'Go home and make amends, and when you honestly consider you have done your duty to your husband, begin to pack your boxes'."

"But don't you believe in love?" asked Mona. "The love that is eternal. The world well lost because the happy possessor has found an affinity?"

"Once in a thousand cases!" was the answer. "The other nine hundred and ninety-nine are infatuations, gilded by sentimentality into romance, romance as described in the kitchen-maids' novelettes, voluptuous kisses, panting breath, and palpitating hearts. Ask your society friends who leave their faithful husbands if they would work for the man of their choice, live alone with him in a two-roomed cottage, willingly forsake amusement and luxury, and be content simply to be with him."

"It would be a severe test," Mona said.

"For a serious decision," he replied gravely. "But I apologise. I've read you a sermon, and it isn't Sunday."

"But you still haven't told me what I am to do," said Mona.

"Trust in the Lord and keep yourself straight until your man is sent back to you."

They sat on in silence until the fire died down and the clock on the mantelpiece struck midnight.

Mona rose.

"Goodnight, and thank you," she said, and clasped the great hand he held out to her.

"God bless you," he said cheerily.

In the sombre bedroom she undressed wearily, glad to creep between the cold sheets and rest, thinking of Peter.

She fell asleep and had a strange dream. She dreamed that she was walking along a path with roses growing on either side in luxuriant profusion, beautiful flowers, wonderfully coloured. But she could not smell their scent, and even as she longed to, came a man, tall and gainly, his face was covered with a veil. He said,

"Come with me and I will take you where the roses are more wonderful, and their perfume a fragrance beyond words."

And she went, but reluctantly, because she loved the path on which she stood. The veiled man led her many weary miles until she found herself in a rocky country, thorny and unfertile. Then he lifted his veil and she saw that the face beneath was exceedingly evil. Terrified, she fled from him and wandered, lonely and afraid, over the desolate land until her feet were sore and bleeding. Then, even as she despaired, wafted on the breeze came the scent of many roses. Desperately she struggled forward. Before her lay the forsaken path of roses, only now their fragrance exceeded all her desires.

"Peter! *Peter!*" she called and woke up.

For a moment she lay wondering at her surroundings, unable to recall where she was. Then Annette entered the room.

"Were you calling, Miss Mona? It is seven o'clock and a lovely morning. The doctor has got the car out and he says we ought to start soon. Then we can spend the night at Harrogate. And it's thankful I shall be to see London," and with this parting shot Annette left Mona to get up.

Her dream had made the future seem full of promise. She rose happily, and twenty minutes later was devouring porridge and chattering gaily to David.

"May I come and see you again?" she asked, "but less informally, I promise you."

"You will always be welcome," he said solemnly.

"I shall use you as a kind of father-confessor," Mona told him. "Bringing my troubles and worries to be erased."

"I shall not always be sympathetic," he threatened, "but my advice will at least be honest."

"That is all I want," she assured him.

Outside a thin wintry sun was trying to peep through the grey clouds. The car stood at the door none the worse for a night in a ditch, save a broken headlight.

"You can get that mended at the next town," said David. "It's not serious."

"How can I thank you for all your kindness?" Mona asked.

"Please don't," he said bashfully. "Only find happiness. Goodbye, little Duchess."

Mona paused in surprise.

"You knew who I was then?"

"I was at school with Peter," he smiled, "and naturally took an interest in the accounts of his marriage. He's the best fellow that ever stepped, and the straightest."

"I know!" answered Mona miserably.

As she drove away she looked back and saw the tall figure silhouetted against the grey house, waving, until they were out of sight.

CHAPTER XXI

The new house was a dream – panelled walls and beautiful old Louis XIV furniture, while all the bedrooms had raised gilt bedsteads hung with silk curtains. Very little alteration was necessary and Mona wondered at the care expended by the last tenant until she learnt her identity.

"An aunt of your husband's," explained the family solicitor when Mona questioned him. "His mother's only sister. The late Duke bought the house for his first wife the year they married and furnished it according to her exquisite taste. When she died, he lent it to her sister for life."

Mona's first feeling was surprise. Peter could not despise her utterly. His mother's house could not be desecrated. She understood how fond the Duchess must have been of these bright rooms, full of her own particular treasures and artistic colourings. The sombre greatness of the castle in Scotland was too vast for alteration, beautiful with the dignity of age. South Street had been a dolls' house. Hardly more than a child, the possession of it had thrilled her. Every wallpaper, each stick of furniture had been planned and arranged. And after all these years the atmosphere was still vital with her laughter-loving personality. It was a house of happiness. For her short-married life had been a time of supreme contentment. Mona could imagine the graceful figure in the gold-and-white drawing room, watching behind the silken curtains for her beloved husband, her face alight with rapture at his return. They were little more than a honeymoon couple and separations of a few hours seemed as long as eternity. Then the knowledge of a little life to come – Peter, whose entry into the world was to mean the sacrifice of his mother's life. But then it was "my baby", and the dreams and tender plans for his future were woven here. There was even a large pink-and-white room at the top of the house prepared for him. Mona could not check her tears beside the cot Peter had never used, the toys he had never played with. For, choosing the date of his birth with a fine disregard for time and place, Peter had been born in Scotland, in an unprepared and gloomy bedroom, and, by the Duke's orders, the house in South Street had been closed for many years.

The hard frost in the country sent all the hunting crowd back to town, and London was full for the *petite saison.* Mona found herself quickly swept into the whirl, asked here and there until her days and nights were planned weeks ahead. She had no time to think and merely lived from hour to hour. Numerous young men attached themselves to her like a kind of retinue. She laughed at their attentions, talking to them like a brother and introducing them to many nice girls. Sally, now very sophisticated and grown-up, showed Mona round with a patronising affected air, which amused her enormously. She had cultivated a languid, vampire-like expression that was ludicrously out of place in Sally's baby face. She feared the effects of too much spoiling until they were alone, when Sally, dropping her mask, became her own natural bright self.

"Isn't this too marvellous, darling, to have you in London again!" she cried enthusiastically. "We will have a hell of a time!"

"Sally!!" remonstrated Mona, pretending to be shocked.

"A hell of a time, *a hell of a time,*" chanted Sally, sprawling on a sofa and showing yards of leg. "And we'll take you to the most wonderful parties. I know a man who makes the strongest cocktails in London."

Mona laughed. She had forgotten the excitement over the latest scandal, trick or eccentricity.

"You are a perfect baby, Sally, in spite of your blasé drawl when you remember it, and those terrible drop earrings."

"Oh, that's the newest pose," Sally answered. "There are four of us – Loo-loo Scorhold, Naomi Grayson, Millicent Hayes and me – and we change our mode of behaviour every month. It's the greatest fun, Mona. Last month we were noisy and hail-fellow-well-met. It was very amusing until Loo-loo imitated Douglas Fairbanks at a private dance and would swing on the candelabrum in the hall. Unluckily it fell down. Loo-loo wasn't hurt, but the chandelier, which apparently was a valuable one, was smashed to atoms and we all had to leave the dance hurriedly. After that we changed our pose to the languid vamp. You must join us, Mona. It's too priceless. Everyone has bets on what our next escapade will be."

"I'm afraid I should not be much good at it," Mona answered, but accepted Sally's invitation to a 'mad' party given by a Count Basarti at his Chelsea studio.

A vast room was painted with queer futuristic pictures in glaring colours, while the lights were shaded by fearsome heads of dragons and gargoyles. Two or three black divans were the only furniture except for a long table containing multi-coloured and peculiar Russian liqueurs in tall glasses. The more conservative cocktail shaker could be observed hidden by a huge bottle of vodka.

The Count was a small man who hid a weak chin behind a well-trimmed beard and his real feelings under a hypocritical mask of insincerity – but for all his affectation he was a wonderful sculptor and his work fetched enormous prices. He had two female models who were always present at his parties. Both were classically hideous, but their ugliness held a weird, almost repulsive, attraction, and their success was remarkable.

Lula, the elder, was not blessed with beauty and had a large mouth and puckered complexion. She wore her hair cut straight in Egyptian fashion and her clothes were practically non-existent. Despite her natural disadvantages she had a great many lovers. Perhaps in these days of degeneration the unusual has a greater power of attraction than the less startling lines of real beauty. How many 'moderns' prefer jazz to Chopin and the Independent Artists to Gainsborough?

The other model would have been an albino save that her eyes were a clear, transparent green, which gave her a remarkable feline appearance that was most disturbing. "She reminds me of one risen from the dead," a famous wag had once remarked, and the description was curiously apt. The colourless skin and hair looked almost lifeless. Only the eyes lived torturously, like fettered souls.

Mona was very much interested. This was a new phase of life and one she had never encountered before. Sally and she went with two men, both in the Brigade of Guards, charming gentlemen in the true sense of the word, but, as types, commonplace. The other guests were certainly far outside that category, artists in strange clothes, talking a still stranger language – women who's white, drawn faces, dilated eyes and nervous hands made one whisper 'drugs' and regard them as strange animals, abnormal and slightly unclean. Society was well represented by dissolute peers, painted women, and girls who seek notoriety regardless of damaged reputations and soiled innocence. Most of Sally's set were present, all accompanied, Mona was glad to see, by presentable young men. She hoped this cult of the disreputable was but a passing phase.

One man, as he entered, struck her forcibly as an undesirable individual. His face, lean and cleanshaven, was pallid with an unhealthy yellow tint, his eyes lined around with a thousand fretwork marks of dissipation, the set firmness of a rather coarse mouth told of a cruel sensuality. He glanced round with an impertinent disdain and saw Mona looking at him. She turned away quickly, but it was too late and, with the lack of convention usual in Chelsea parties, he crossed to her side.

"May I welcome a newcomer to our midst?" he asked, and his voice, strange and husky, was in keeping with his appearance.

"Thank you." Mona bowed coldly and continued her conversation with Sally, who was sitting next to her, but unluckily Sally knew him and had an axe to grind.

"Mr. Sangtama, when are you going to paint my portrait?"

"You are too pink and white for my brushes, Miss Sally," he answered. "Ask Serge. Being a Russian, he likes the Teuton fairness." Disregarding Sally's pouts he turned to Mona. "But I will paint you, little lady. Why not as Daphne fleeing from Apollo? Have you no pursuing lover to make you feel the part?"

Mona flushed at the impertinence and, without realising the fame of the painter and the underlying compliment in his offer, rose with dignity.

"I'm afraid I have no spare time to sit as your model," she answered and walked away, missing the gleam of anger in Sangtama's eyes and the tightening of the cruel mouth.

Later in the evening the fun waxed fast and furious. They danced, the music supplied by a pianist who had been applauded by crowned heads. They acted, absurd impromptu sketches, clever in their sheer buffoonery, and they drank – one after another of the coloured liqueurs, while the shaker 'shimmied' unceasingly the whole evening. At last, in the early hours of the morning, the Count, slightly unsteady on his feet, clapped his hands and suggested a "General Post Dance". When the music stopped they were all to change partners before it went on again. A childish game, but it amused the motley crowd.

Mona from the arms of her partner saw Sangtama edging towards her and, when the music stopped, she separated from Archie Fellows for but one second and then joined him again.

"Unfair!" Sangtama shouted, but the music started and they danced away from him.

Suddenly the room was plunged in darkness. For a moment there was a gasp of astonishment, then everyone laughed and shrieked with amusement. Figures running away or being pursued bumped against each other blindly and Mona was separated from Archie. She tried to grope her way to the side of the room, but at every turn came up against an embracing or struggling couple. Quite unexpectedly a hand grasped her arm and before she could move touched her face. Furious, she fought for her freedom, but was picked up off her feet and carried along like a baby.

"Let me down!" she cried angrily, but a chuckle was her only answer and she guessed it was Sangtama. She struggled desperately and fiercely, but she was like clay in the hands of this tall man. He even treated her resistance as a joke, laughing quietly at the blows she dealt him as he bore her across the room. She felt him open a door and, passing through, close it behind him, and knew they were in another room, empty to judge by the quietness.

"Now," he said," what are you going to do about it, little spitfire!"

"Put me down!" Mona commanded.

"Not so fast, *ma chère*. You've got to apologise first."

She could feel his breath on her face and knew in one moment he would kiss her. Only by a trick could she escape and her brain worked quickly.

"All right, you win," she made her voice natural and pleasant. "Only for goodness' sake open a window or I shall faint in the heat."

He carried her across the room and set her on the wide sill. Then he started to pull down the heavy window. Like a flash Mona was on the floor and pulling open the door. He was only just behind her, so she slammed it to again, remaining inside. There would have been no time to slip through herself, but there was just a chance that he would be deceived and go straight out into the studio without turning on the lights. A chance – and it turned up! Sangtama rushed through the door and Mona, shutting it softly after him, turned the key in the lock. She refused to face the crowd again. Still giggling in the darkness and now playing a silly game of hide-and-seek, the penalty of being caught being the forfeit of a kiss, hurriedly she opened the window at the bottom and looked out. There was a drop of about six feet into a yard, which led into the street.

Mona clambered out, swung for a terrifying moment, then dropped, none the worse except for a ruined dress, owing to the fact that the corner of the yard had been used to stack coal. She opened the street gate and looked outside. A little further up the road she saw Sally and her escort walking down the front-door steps into a taxi. With a little "Holloa" she ran towards them.

"Why, darling," said Sally, "I thought you must have gone home. I called you, but it was impossible to find anyone. Why, look at your dress."

"Coal," answered Mona with a little grimace. "I've been getting close to nature."

"We've certainly had a dose of it tonight," Sally laughed at her sarcasm, "and I've lost a diamond brooch. I think our next pose, Archie, will be pickpocketing. It's a lucrative pursuit."

"God forbid!" he said piously, ostentatiously removing his watch from the pocket nearest her.

CHAPTER XXII

Raymond Power was the most notorious young man in London. At the age of twenty-eight he had collected a reputation worthy of the dandies of the Georgian era.

He positively revelled in the ostracism of the dowagers and the frightened, half-fascinated flutterings of *débutantes* when he asked them for a dance. As a matter of fact his bark was far worse than his bite, but society always judges by the face value of its victim, and Raymond was given the credit of every anonymous escapade and the credit of each exaggerated story of his actions.

Like a lot of notabilities his supposed character was the most interesting thing about him. The real man was only a rather dull small boy playing a game of desperado. Yet like all women Mona was attracted to the bold, bad buccaneer, and when she met Raymond at a party and he asked her to go out with him, she accepted out of pure curiosity.

Raymond called at South Street about eight o'clock and Mona, dressed in a frock of deep orange georgette with a bunch of mauve orchids pinned to her shoulder, was waiting.

"You look topping!" he said appraisingly.

But Mona, who had expected a rhapsody from this *petit roué* or a delicately witty compliment, merely laughed. What a child this much-talked-of young man was, giving utterance to his admiration like any schoolboy, yet apparently holding the good name of many beautiful women in the hollow of his hand or, more literally, behind sealed lips.

But he was intelligent, this *jeune* Don Juan, and dining at the embassy she found herself interested, in spite of the transparency to her, of his pose.

"It's a pity you can't be indiscreet discreetly," she told him as the Duchess of Minster met his bow with a cold stare and minute inclination of her tiaraed head.

"Where do you draw the line between discretion and deceit?" he questioned.

"Discretion is camouflage, the art of showing a well-powdered nose to the world, while deceit is an underhand and unpleasant evasion of the truth."

"I see no connection," he protested. "Indiscretion is merely the pleasant word with which we cloak our own licentiousness. Our neighbours have other and perhaps more explicit terms of description, especially if I am the subject of discussion," he added, laughing.

"I believe you glory in your bad reputation," accused Mona.

"Most people prefer to be talked about unkindly than not mentioned at all! Some people are born notorious, some attain notoriety, and some make themselves notorious," he misquoted, "Behold in me the latter."

"Change the word to 'foolish'," answered Mona.

"Foolishness, my dear," he replied, "merely consists in doing something unpleasant to yourself or something you will regret afterwards. Living from day to day is not foolishness, it is refusal to speculate on the future. Treasure in Heaven is not a gilt-edged security. It is an unknown quantity. Likewise, tomorrow is a gamble, for who knows what tomorrow will bring?"

"What a vagabond creed!" Mona laughed. "A wandering traveller!"

"Will you join my journeyings?" he asked, bending towards her.

"Do they lead to Eldorado" she asked.

"Arcady," he corrected, "the ideal paradise!"

The word brought back a little pang of remembrance, the white bungalow on the green hills, was *'he'* there now and was she missed? There was, more than likely, someone to take her place. One could not live alone in Arcadia. Curiously enough the thought did not hurt her and for a moment she was surprised at herself. Then the explanation seemed simple and clear. She was regretting but the trappings of happiness, coveting but the beautiful frame of a picture, and quite suddenly she realised that Arcadia consists in the blending of two people into one – that the scenery, seductive and atmospheric, is really but the creation of their imagination. Hell together can be Utopia, while Paradise apart seems but the cesspool of damnation.

"Those whom God hath joined together…"

The words came hauntingly. "Together..." She felt cynical and bitter. A tiny unsatisfied ache told her how much she wanted Peter, the comfort of his love and the restfulness of his presence. She was as a ship without a rudder, whirled hither and thither by the winds of chance, journeying – where? Then pride raised its head and scorned the softening of her heart.

'I don't care,' she told herself, and smiled into the dark eyes of her companion, which responded all too quickly to the encouragement.

Dinner finished, they rose to go to a theatre. Raymond had taken a box at the latest revue. They had missed half the performance, but Mona felt it was the atmosphere of gaiety she needed. Recklessly she was flirting with

Raymond, murmuring “Hush” to his more daring remarks, but egging him on with teasing side-glances and half-smiles.

In the seclusion of the box he insisted on holding her hand, and for a moment she felt his lips on her bare shoulder.

“Do behave,” she admonished him.

“I can’t with you,” he retorted.” You maddeningly, adorable creature!”

“I shall leave you,” she threatened half-seriously.

“Oh no, you won’t,” he replied. “You are mine for tonight.” He said the last words insistently and a thrill of fear seized Mona.

Then she laughed.

“You flatter yourself, *cher* Raymond.”

“You will be kind, please.” He whispered the words, yet their quietness held a fierceness, a deep roar of desire, and her fingers were crushed by the hard grip of his.

She hesitated coquettishly and at that moment the lights went up.

“Answer me!” commanded Raymond.

“Well...” she prevaricated, then stopped, her heart beating wildly, her pulses throbbing with sickening intensity. Below in the stalls sat Peter. For a moment the theatre swam. Only Peter’s face remained visible, his hair smooth-brushed, his eyes twinkling with laughter.

Laughing! And Mona looked immediately for his companion, then received a shock. Peter was with a woman. The first infuriating feelings of jealousy! Tall and fair, a daughter of Juno, light blue eyes, fringed with darkened lashes.

'I expect Peter thinks them natural,' came the catty thought. 'Red mouth pouting provocatively over pearly teeth, white shoulders gleaming against a black dress,'

'Temptress! *I hate her,*' cried Mona in her heart, resisting the primal impulse to rush down and hit the usurper, to pull the golden hair, to slap the pink-and-white cheeks until they burned red and bruised, then to take away Peter, *her* Peter! And this woman was making him laugh. Damn her, damn her, *damn her!*

Mona almost sobbed aloud with anger. Then, sitting stiffly in the box, she fancied she saw herself acting a part, her swift movements to reach the stalls, felt the shrinking flesh of the terrified woman she drove from Peter's side, watched the fair face whiten, the bright eyes contracted, saw Peter watching her in astonishment as she flung passionate arms around him. She felt the soft warmth of his coat against her face as she dropped her head on his shoulder, saw his eyes when she raised her mouth to his, fierce and cruel as when he had left her, yet hungry with unsatisfied desire that thrilled her whole body – and she heard herself say,

"I love you, Peter!" and watched the change in his face, the...

"Answer me!" The dream broke as the strange voice dragged Mona back to consciousness. Only a few seconds had passed, yet seared their passing on her heart with brands of fire. Mona looked at Raymond in a dazed manner. Why was she with this man? She wanted to be alone to realise the revelation that was crying in her brain, throbbing in her breast. The truth at last! She loved Peter, loved him beyond all imagination or the pretensions of cheap imitations. She wanted to cry out, to make Peter realise, to compel his attention across the crowd of strangers, these fools who watched love portrayed on the stage when a real drama was being enacted among them. Peter, *Peter!*

But Peter was hers no longer. Perhaps this other woman rested in the security of his arms, enjoyed the comfort of his consideration and unfailing kindness. H*er* husband, hers by right, and she had thrown away a treasure beyond price in grasping at a shadow.

'I will have him back, *I will!*' Primitive woman, love, willing compliance to her desire, demanded her mate. But she could not meet him now, nor receive a chilly bow across a space that seemed a great fixed gulf – the chasm of our appearances in public, which must ever be circumspect, even if our hearts are breaking.

Without any explanation Mona rose.

"I want to go home."

She hardly heard Raymond's expostulations – she must get away and think. His pleadings, entreaties, blustering, fell on deaf ears. Taking one last look at Peter, Mona, with an aching misery in her heart, left the theatre.

CHAPTER XXIII

What excuse could she make for seeing Peter? For weeks the question went unanswered, turned over and over, round and round, unceasingly in Mona's brain. Each solution when scrutinised seemed impracticable or impossible, and the days dragged by like giant shadows, intangible, immaterial, while the nights were tossing centuries of wakefulness or delirious dreams.

Even Annette wore a worried expression as she watched her beloved mistress grow thinner and whiter, but she said nothing aloud, only muttered curses on the head of the absent Alec as she took pleats in Mona's clothes, which daily grew too large for comfort.

Christmas passed, an unjoyous festival at South Street save in the servants' hall. And the New Year arrived unwelcomed.

'One needs children,' thought Mona as, alone in the silent house, she watched from the window a crowd of schoolboys pelting each other with snowballs, laughing and gambolling like young fauns. Even the joy of motherhood was to be denied to her and the hideous loneliness of the future loomed larger and more frightening. Society began to creep back to town, many only packing their boxes *en route* for the South, the rest craving a little hectic amusement after a dull sojourn in the country. Mona found her days filled with engagements, useless, petty, boring engagements, but they took her thoughts away from herself and forced a pretended forgetfulness that was mentally beneficial even though unrecognised by the beneficiary.

Sally returned from a visit to Leicestershire and came round to see Mona, bringing into the dull house a spirit of *jeunesse*. Her bright face, invigorated by the frosty air, her light laughter, made Mona smile even when she most wanted to indulge in self-pity. Sally dropped into an easy chair and crossed her silk-clad legs, causing her short tight skirt to recede alarmingly.

"A cigarette, darling," she gasped, "and don't ask me how the hunting is! If anyone mentions that particular sport again, I'll scream! I've had the subject undiluted for three weeks. At breakfast I've discussed the prospects of a good run, at lunch – consisting of two mouldy sandwiches – I've watched the good run, at dinner. I've listened to descriptions of every inch of the good run and gone to bed early in hopes of a good run on the morrow! God!!!"

Mona laughed.

"*Pauvre enfant!* And not a flirtation all the time?"

"One with a devotee of the chase. When he wasn't hunting, he was drinking, and I was squeezed into the intervals when there were any! To forsake hunting will be a clause on my marriage contract."

"What are your plans for the immediate future?" asked Mona, "apart from your matrimonial intentions."

"A party, my child, at which your presence is imperative. We will start at eight-thirty and be returned *chez-nous* with the morning's milk."

Mona demurred for a few seconds, but Sally allowed no refusal and presently departed as noisily and as hurriedly as she had arrived, but holding Mona's promise to be ready at eight-twenty-five when she was "called for".

'What does it matter either way?' thought Mona miserably as she went up to change. Later she lay in her bath, staring at the green ceiling, remembering an evening on their honeymoon when Peter had carried her into the bathroom and, regardless of her protestations, had dropped her into the water with a splash, only laughing when she scolded him for wetting her hair.

"If ever you annoy me," he had threatened, "I shall seize this long silky stuff and drag you away by it to my lair!" She remembered how she had experienced a tiny poignant thrill, a primitive feminine appreciation of brutality from a possessive lover – and how she had realised the absurdity of a feeling, almost of disappointment, when her shy "Not really, Peter!" had been answered by a gentle kiss and "I wouldn't hurt a hair of your blessed head, darling".

How blind men were! They quoted endlessly the hackneyed phrases – a woman, a dog, and a walnut tree – 'catch 'em young, treat 'em rough'. Yet in real life they never materialised their sentiments. Women, according to psycho-analysts, might be spiritually superior to the male sex, but they were a thousand times humbler in their emotions, hungrier in their lusts and less easily satisfied because their brain plays as active a part in their desires as the body. They are unlike the man who is carried away by a wave of passion and is then uninterested and normal when the moment is past. Very few women, especially in the modern age, are 'swept off their feet'. That time-worn phrase, beloved of Victorians, is really but a weak excuse for licentiousness or seriously contemplated abandon. For women do nothing without the consent of the mind, and with that concession goes the defence of uncontrollable subordination.

A white numbness about the tips of her fingers told Mona she had been too long in the water, and she got out onto the soft bathmat, wrapping herself in the large rough towel that was laid ready over the chair. The friction of drying made her blood tingle to the surface and the feeling of physical well-being lightened her mental depression. By the time she was ready to dress, her mood had changed to one of cheerful anticipation.

Sally arrived, twenty minutes late, in a huge car crammed with chattering juvenile humanity.

"We had to stop at various houses on the way for cocktails," she excused her lateness, and introduced everyone by their Christian or nicknames.

Mona knew about three of the people and for the rest she received a jumbled impression of Fudge a plump young man with horn-rimmed glasses, Gladys, a slight girl with feverish dilated eyes, whom she recognised as the younger daughter of a socialist earl and whose amours and *affaires* were not only the talk of every Mayfair drawing room, but were of vital interest in the kitchen, and to the suburban purchasers of the libellous newspapers that specialise in society gossip. Odol, the conceited one, possessed a handsome row of white teeth and a notoriously unclean mind and Bonzo was an unpretentious youth with an incredibly large bank balance and a high-sounding title. They crowded in somehow and drove noisily to the Embassy.

Mona was indisputably the success of the party. Her wit flashed and sparkled as irresistibly as her eyes, and her laughter was as hard to withstand as an invitation to drink. The conversation was as bewildering as the amusements park at Wembley. No subject held the fickle interest for long. The next side-show attracted, even before the possibilities of the one they regarded first had been explored.

"Look at this!" someone cried, and away they rushed, the platitudes and youthful bromides as ancient as the hoop-las and lucky Derbies that call themselves "novelties". About twelve o'clock they decided to move somewhere else, but Mona, rising from the table, suddenly stopped short and stared at the doorway, standing as though made of graven stone. Just inside, glancing nonchalantly round the room, immaculately dressed and criticising the dancers with an insufferable air of cynicism, was Alec.

For a moment the noise of the room receded dizzily into the distance and every vestige of colour drained from her face. Then, with a supreme effort, Mona drained her glass of champagne and turned to face his recognition, apparently unmoved.

"Mona!" His hand clasped hers and his touch but accentuated the numbness which was creeping over her. Frozen to every emotion, she answered his greetings with doll-like precision and introduced him to her party. She watched the instantaneous effect of his charms on Sally's susceptibilities and as in a dream heard him accept an invitation to join their table. Only when Alec turned to her with a question did life move again in her veins, and then the quickening emotion was one of surprise. With his old smile of a thousand unspoken insinuations, Alec said,

"And how is the perfect husband, O faithful Undine?"

He did not know. And with a flash of fear Mona realised that at all costs her separation from Peter must remain a secret for tonight, Alec must be ignorant until tomorrow, when she could leave London or refuse to see him. And even while she knew this course to be imperative, she wondered at her own acknowledgment of its importance. For surely the incitement to 'run away' from Alec was an ironical trick of Fate, when only a few months before she had been ready to 'run with' him.

Then, as all truths about ourselves become known to us in a flash of clear insight, which is the supremacy of the brain over the emotions that have clogged the mechanism of unbiased judgment, came a revelation to Mona. Her infatuation for Alec was dead – dead beyond revival or resurrection, and out of the ashes of her first awakening emotions had risen, phoenix-like, her love for Peter, growing until it culminated in this moment, when all else was dross beside the glory in her heart that was yet an agony because she was alone. Woman-like she wished to hide her conception. She feared the prying eyes and chattering tongues, poisonous with curiosity. And she shrank from Alec. His uncanny mesmeric powers might tear her secret from her. Secure with a mooring from which nothing could tear her, there was still to be feared further efforts of seduction from Alec, who would consider her elopement with him was but postponed by the Duke's death, and that she had been an unwilling victim of unforeseen events, which had dragged her back to her husband's side. Like startled rabbits her thoughts ran hither and thither. Then with an effort she remembered that Alec awaited an answer to his question. With perfect control in her voice, she answered carelessly,

"Peter is very hearty – he will be interested to hear of your return."

But even as she spoke, she saw the mocking laughter in Alec's face and realised her supposition of his ignorance was but a fool's paradise. Alec was perfectly informed and only playing with her as a cat with a mouse, watching with cynical amusement the transparent deception with which she tried to blind him to the truth.

Although Mona dreaded the moment when Alec would show his hand, she felt within herself a veritable tower of defence, an inviolable sanctuary that nothing would or could desecrate, nothing destroy, a stronghold against the wiles of a temptation which tempted no longer, a fort that would surrender only to the rightful commander, and even if uncoveted by him would remain faithful, even unto death.

Without a tremor save that her face was still pale, she faced Alec proudly.

"So you know!" he challenged. "Plucky little Undine!" he prevaricated, his voice caressing as the wind stirring among baby fir trees.

"Don't be a beast, Alec," Mona answered unexpectedly. "I'm full of self-pity, but jam is a poor substitute for iced cake."

"So!" Alec raised his eyebrows. "And I am not to be allowed even to offer chocolate creams as a *sucredouceur*"

"Yours are of a very inferior chocolate, Alec," Mona replied.

"You didn't think that once," Alec retorted quietly, but the fire in his dark eyes made Mona aware of his anger and resentment. The others rose for "just one more dance", and under cover of their retreat she made one last appeal, holding out her hand to Alec.

Hastily she changed the subject.

"You didn't go to Jamaica."

"I left the boat at Marseilles. My stipulation for Paradise included thou,' an item apparently forgotten in the haste of embarkation."

"So you have returned..." Mona faltered.

"For you!"

They faced each other gravely. Their eyes met. And in that moment Mona knew Alec meant to fight her last resistance. There was to be no mercy, no quarter.

"I am very lonely, for a friend."

"And I am very lonely, for you," he retorted, quelling Mona's hopes roughly. "You have wilfully lost everything now."

"Except my soul," she quoted, trying to laugh lightly and failing miserably. Two great tears welled up in her eyes, blinding her sight with their reflecting glitter.

"If you cry, I shall kiss you." Alec's voice was normal and bantering again.

"And be removed for immorality," Mona answered in the same vein.

Oh, the rigidness of the unwritten code of *noblesse oblige*, the mask of superficial immobility, which may not be dropped.

A couple at the next table rose to dance, an ill-bred, overdressed woman escorted by a clothes-horse that called itself a man, with long side whiskers and a gardenia buttonhole that vied with the unhealthy pallor of his face. As the woman abandoned herself to his flabby arms, she stared curiously at Mona, then turned to her companion, and her remark was perfectly audible.

"The Duchess of Glenac! They've been parted some time, but she seems to be consoling herself.

Consoling herself! Oh, Peter, *Peter!*

Mona rose.

"I am going home Alec – alone."

How she said goodbye, what she said, or how she refused Alec's entreaties, Mona was not consciously aware. She knew only an overwhelming desire for solitude, to escape from the curious faces around her and the naked hunger in Alec's eyes. She wanted to run, and run, and run.

"Goodbye, Alec." She gave him her hand and shivered slightly as she felt his lips.

"*Au revoir* Undine – till tomorrow."

His words were meaningly distinct and she sank back against the cushions of the car as though in search of protection.

She wanted to run, and run, and run…

CHAPTER XXIV

ONE, two, three, four, five, six! The clock on the Grosvenor Chapel struck slowly as though forced against its will to tell the truth up to the last stroke.

Mona turned on the lights, for it was still dark, and slipped out of bed. She started to dress, then, after a few minutes, rang the bell. A startled under-housemaid, flushed and sleepy, appeared, disturbed from an early cup of tea in the kitchen before starting her labours in the house.

"Tell Annette I want her as soon as she can be dressed and bring me some breakfast as soon as possible."

"Very good, your Grace," and the wide-eyed domestic disappeared to inform her fellow-servants that "something was up".

By the time Annette had been aroused, Mona was dressed and had begun to pack her dressing-case.

"Annette, we are going to Paris," she told the faithful maid who entered, full of anxiety and perturbed by the unusualness of such early rising.

"Today, Miss Mona?"

"This morning," answered Mona firmly, sensing an argument in Annette's disapproving face. "Please pack a box and give orders that no one is to be given my address. We will catch the eight forty-five train from Victoria."

Realising the futility of opposition, Annette, with a few sniffs, left the room.

'Poor Annette!' Mona smiled. 'Travelling is her *bête noire.*'

Calmly she ate a hearty breakfast – there were adventures ahead and all the excitement of a childish game of hide-and-seek.

At a quarter to eight, amid a flurry of last-minute packing and belated instructions, Mona and Annette started for the station and, having had the forethought to telephone to the Station Master, found two seats reserved for them on a train crowded by holidaymakers bound for the winter sports in Switzerland and early voyagers to Cannes and Monte Carlo.

Their fellow passengers were amusing to watch, the fat, flustered females, who hurried the porters in high-pitched, screeching voices, clad in the hideous ill-fitting tweeds that have become a universal joke as an Englishwoman's uniform abroad. There were, however, several exponents of the opposite extreme in dress. One girl, in particular, wore a velvet *toque* massed in pale blue ostrich feathers and sported diamond buckles on her high-heeled suede shoes. The men were mostly stamped with an air of business, a small leather dispatch case completed their luggage, and the papers under their arms bore the magic word 'financial' somewhere in their titles.

Each voyager found his seat in the train and attempted to procure a carriage for himself alone. Later arrivals received black looks but united against other intruders, until the last person to enter had the combined enmity of the whole carriage. It was like a round game, the last home forfeiting his comfort.

The sea was rough and unprepossessing, so Annette retired immediately to lie down. One by one the female passengers left the deck green in the face, and yawning with the awful sickly continuance that denotes the beginning of *mal de mer*. It was too cold to sit down, a keen wind pierced its way into every corner. Mona walked briskly up and down, wrapping her fur coat closely around her. After half an hour or so it commenced to rain, and even the male element dispersed to the smoking-room or bar. The deck became unpleasantly wet, but Mona could not face the close confinement of a cabin or the hot oily smell below. After a while, roused from her thoughts, she became conscious of the scrutiny of a fellow passenger, and for the first time noticed a tall, heavily built man who was also pacing the deck. His face was vaguely familiar and as she looked at him, he crossed to her side, holding out his hand.

"Have you forgotten me?" he questioned.

"Only your name and occupation!" Mona smiled.

"The latter is negligible and the former unimportant," he answered, "so you are forgiven. But you danced with me three times at the Stanhopes' dance."

The Stanhopes! The night she became engaged to Peter, when her misery had been too intense to allow the remembrance of anything save anguish and the escape Peter offered from terrible bogies which had been mostly of her own imagination. And this man – vaguely through the films of memory came a shadowy reminiscence of kindly sympathy from one partner that ghastly evening. The familiarity of his face recurred and fitted into the recollection.

"Of course, I remember you now," said Mona.

"And you still look sad!" he interpolated.

"Today I am happy. I'm running away from all my troubles – bound for Paris, which is like going home for me."

"You can't run away from trouble. It travels faster than any human agency, so it is invariably in front of you unless you conquer it," he said half seriously, half-laughingly.

"You have *mettre de l'eau dans son vin*," Mona teased, and they both laughed.

At Calais, amid the excitement of disembarkation, Mona noticed the label on his suitcase.

"Viscount Courtley."

Instantly she recollected a conversation between her mother and an erstwhile beautiful woman, spending the fleeting years in collecting scandal in much the same way as small boys collect stamps or cigarette cards.

"Eric Courtley is living with her at the moment," had been the latest gem. "But Goldstein won't divorce her because her settlements are too large."

Harriet Goldstein, a beautiful American, had married Nathan Goldstein for his money and, having a clever business head, had seen that the marriage settlements were favourable whatever her behaviour or her husband's line of action. Six months after her marriage she had fallen desperately in love with the penniless Courtley, heir to an Irish earldom and acres of worthless estates. Nathan refused divorce, so Harriet bought a palatial flat in Paris, where she entertained largely and made a comfortable home for her lover.

Courtley amused Mona on the rather tiring train journey to Paris. He had the inevitable Irish sense of humour, which finds amusement in the most commonplace occurrence. He made her laugh at incidents that had she been alone would have merely annoyed her. He mimicked their fellow passengers and insisted on smiling at the girl with the diamond buckles who had reappeared rather paler than before but with the ostrich feathers still flying bravely.

"She is one of those freaks of nature," he told Mona, "especially created by the Almighty for the laughter of man. Any attention she believes is admiration, so she is supremely happy. Do you know Paris well?" he asked more seriously.

"I was at school here and love it dearly," Mona answered. "Don't you?"

"To me Paris is a beautiful woman," Courtley answered. "She has a thousand moods, innumerable airs and graces. One adores her, anticipating every whim. But just occasionally one longs for Ireland. A frosty morning, a horse, and a good run! That is a better life than poodle-faking."

Mona laughed, but she heard the longing in his voice. Harriet Goldstein must be a very clever woman, she thought, to hold him. Few women are strong enough to keep men from sport and sometimes business. The wise ones make no attempt.

"I can't stand a man lounging about the house all day!" they say, convincing their friends, and occasionally themselves.

At the Gare du Nord, Courtley asked for Mona's address and bade her an elaborate farewell, without offering to accompany her to her destination. Outside the station stood a closed-in car, polished and glistening, like a well-groomed horse, a chauffeur in an ornate livery holding the door. As Courtley appeared, a white bejewelled hand fluttered at the window.

As Mona had said, returning to Paris was for her a homecoming. The vivacious excitement of the passers-by, the hurrying noisy traffic, the houses with their green shutters invitingly open, welcomed her like a maternal embrace. It was cold, but with the sharp invigorating chill of dry frosty air, and every now and then a sun would gleam from the sky, lighting on the smiling faces in the crowded streets.

On the way from the station one incident struck her as being typical of French life. A poorly dressed girl, but nevertheless with the chic of her class, was waiting to cross the street. A florist's assistant, to judge by the bunch of carnations she held in her arms, addressed, no doubt, to the *amour* of some amorous French boy. There is something very young about the choice of red carnations. At last, tiring of waiting for the traffic to be held up, the gendarme was engaged in conversation, the *petite Parisienne* seized her opportunity and sped across the road, under the bonnets of cars that did not slacken their speed, perilously near the heavy buses. Breathlessly but unscathed she gained the pavement, but in her haste two crimson blossoms lay in the mud. Gaily she abandoned them, but the gendarme, suddenly active, tore himself away from his interesting friend. Shrilly he blew his whistle, holding out his absurd little truncheon. As the traffic came to a standstill he stepped into the centre of the street, picked up the carnations and placed them in his cap. Cheerily he smiled at his friend. *"De bonne augure, Pierre,"* then, with a wave of his hand, he bade the traffic proceed.

Mona procured rooms at the Ritz, an unusually easy procedure, as Paris was comparatively empty. She was helping Annette unpack when the telephone rang and she heard Courtley's deep well-bred voice on the wire.

"I wondered if you would dine with us tonight, Duchess, and meet Mrs. Goldstein."

Normally Mona would have refused, not because she objected to the looseness of Mrs. Goldstein's morals, but the lady in question would doubtless bore her with an overdose of voluble and accented reminisces of America. Still, a lonely dinner is a poor antidote to a threatened attack of depression, and Paris without companions is the loneliest city in the world. So Mona answered the invitation in the affirmative and Courtley rejoiced.

"My standards of propriety are becoming lax," said Mona to Annette. "Which is neither here nor there, but interesting to note, in that some people would call it broad-minded – which but goes to show that every opinion has an opposite."

This conversation being unintelligible to Annette, she merely said,

"Yes, your Grace," and continued unpacking.

But Mona was arguing with herself, an unending and unprofitable pursuit, yet one that, once started, persistently continues until a climax or conclusion is reached.

'And is Harriet Goldstein worse than any of us?' she queried. 'She is at least honest with herself, her husband, her lover, and the world, while we hide our dirt with face-powder, cover our lousy heads with pretentious hats, blind our acquaintances with a dazzling smile of false teeth and deceive the man in the street, while our peers forgive and condone any game where the rules of sport are observed!'

"What dress will your Grace wear this afternoon?" Annette's voice was full of rebuke and disapproval. She considered morals better left undiscussed.

Mona changed from the severe tailor-made lines of her travelling suit into clothes that would pass muster in the city of beautiful clothes and journeyed towards St. Cloud. She determined that her first hours in Paris should be spent in a visit to the Convent de Sacré Coeur.

'Only a year has passed,' she thought, as she sped through the Bois in the swift automobile. 'Yet so much has happened. Mona of the peaceful heart has gone, gone with the golden ideals and severe judgments of right and wrong, and in her place ... is nothing – merely the outside walls of an empty building, the husk and rind of what was once fruit of great promise.'

Sensitive, she craved more than the sincere but dignified welcome accorded her by the nuns and pupils at the convent. They were so complete in the security of their sheltered life, busy with their own interests, demanding so little that they were invariably content.

Mona felt an alien in their midst, only a visitor, where she wished to belong. The convent was not the warm loving mother she desired and remembered, but a cold emblem of maternity, as unreal as the statue in the chapel of the Mother of God. But Mona quelled the criticism of her brain and tried to fill her heart with the old welling affection. She lit a candle before each flower-laden shrine, the Blessed Virgin, the Holy Family, St. Anthony – who will restore missing possessions.

"And I have lost a husband," Mona told the little Saint whimsically, then lit yet another candle on the glittering stand.

Outside the chapel in the grey cloisters the Abbess awaited her, a tall woman, beautiful with a spiritual beauty which made one instinctively listen attentively when she spoke and obey her slightest command. Her story was a sad one. The only child of an aristocratic French family which had fallen on evil days, her *début* made a stir in the small circle of their remaining friends. Within a month she had two suitors, one the penniless son of an impoverished marquis, the other a youthful owner of a valuable factory. The former was good-looking, chivalrous and graceful, with all the charm of the old *régime,* but his rival had the thick coarse figure of the bourgeois, and the arrogant characteristics of a self-made man.

The young *débutante* was in despair. Against her heart was balanced the salvation of the family fortunes. But she was not consulted. A marriage was arranged with her wealthy suitor, disobedience to her family an unthought-of possibility. A week before the ceremony a distant relative left her father a large legacy – her sacrifice would be in vain, but her word had been given, and the *noblesse* did not break a promise, even to the bourgeois. The day before the nuptials were to be celebrated, Denise de Calincourt entered the Convent de Sacré Coeur and became Sister Cecilia, leaving behind an infuriated fiancé and a broken-hearted lover. Her own sufferings made her wonderfully sympathetic with young girls, and she was worried now by the look of tired sadness in Mona's pale face.

"You have no children?" she questioned her late charge, her own barren spinsterhood making her long to hear of the pregnancy of others.

"No!" Mona's voice was unknowingly bitter.

"But there is plenty of time," said the gentle woman. "You are very young, my child."

Mona felt an overwhelming desire to tell the Abbess her troubles, to pour forth her woes, as when a child she had brought her petty sorrows and tiny tragedies which had then seemed enormous to the unfailing sympathy and advice of one who, as a priestess of a God of Love, judged all things from the standpoint of Mercy and Kindliness.

Yet even as the thought came to her, it was contradicted by a second. The narrowness of convent life was not the best medium for implanting an understanding of the temptations of Mammon. Only experience could teach their validity, only one who had conquered could advise another's tactics in the eternal warfare.

Even peace among the old associations was to be denied her. She belonged outside, to the faint roar of the world, wafting over the green fields of St. Cloud, as indistinct as the buzzing of an insect, but to Mona a clarion call to return *aux armes.* "Of a fighting age!" The phrase of wartime made her smile. That was the class to which she belonged. Here were the schoolchildren training as cadets, instructed by a past generation, C3 on the army records, their services necessary but not compulsory. And all through the centuries the battles would continue, had continued.

As the chapel bell tolled for Benediction, Mona took the road back to Paris, back to her worries, difficulties, and misgivings, but filled with a new courage, refreshed ambitions.

Dusk was beginning to fall, a purple darkness creeping over the city.

'Prendre la lune avec les dents,' Mona encouraged herself, but there was a suspicious break in the quiet voice.

CHAPTER XXV

"I'm so glad you could come." Courtley grasped Mona's hand and drew her into the brightly decorated drawing room of Harriet Goldstein's *appartement.* Masses of mauve orchids gave a look of opulence, which was accentuated by the embossed gold mirrors and ornate French furniture. Rose-shaded lights and silk curtains created an atmosphere of sensuous voluptuousness, while the faint sickly scent of an Eastern perfume pervaded everything. Harriet Goldstein mixed a tendency for reckless extravagance with a craving for luxury, a taste that, fostered by her husband, had become a passion. It was a relief to turn the eyes to the heavy, sombre outlines of Courtley, retaining among these feminine trappings the clean outdoor air that is peculiar to the public-schooled English and sport-loving Irish.

Before Mona had time for more than a fleeting impression of her surroundings, Harriet Goldstein entered. Taller than the average, she was so thin that one expected with every movement to see a bone thrust through the white skin – white as after a long illness with the blue veins showing like innumerable railroads. Her face was long and pointed, with a crimson gash for a mouth, which curved when she smiled like a sleepy snake. Her eyes, heavily pencilled, were dark and feverish. One felt they never rested, never closed. It seemed almost indelicate to look at them, they revealed so much of the restless hungry soul locked between those pointed breasts. Even her voice diffused hunger. It was deep and low, with every now and then a raw note behind the measured tones.

"How kind of you to come!" she purred over Mona, touching her with an icy cold hand. "And the Prince?" She turned to Courtley.

"Will be here in a few minutes," he answered.

"You know Prince Kahnna?"

Mona shook her head.

"He is charming," her hostess continued, yet her eyes seemed to laugh ironically at some abstruse joke. "Egyptian and so absurdly rich, and wicked! That man is capable of any devilment."

"My dear!" Courtley spoke almost sharply.

"But why pretend?" The light glittered on the long nails of the gesticulating hand. "I adore wickedness, as some people adore drink. It intoxicates me. The Prince has greater capabilities for evil than anyone I know. So, he adorns my collection." She turned to Mona. "My dear, I'm not entirely heinous, for Courtley is the exception to all my infamies."

Mona laughed. This woman interested her enormously.

Courtley went to the end of the room to mix a cocktail and for the moment was out of hearing. Harriet fitted a fresh cigarette into her black onyx holder and bent towards Mona.

"I think it was sweet of you to come here, Duchess. I bet Courtley you wouldn't come when he wanted to invite you."

"It was so kind of you to ask me" Mona was nonplussed and rather embarrassed.

"My dear!" Harriet gave a short deep laugh. "You may call a woman like me a courtesan or a tart. One is generally taken to mean the mistress of a King and the other, in *le langage des halles*, means 'fourpence and a beer'. But their creeds are much the same, and the virtuous to show their virtue must cross the street. There, I've shocked you, *mais, que voulez vous?*"

Mona was spared an answer, for at that moment the Prince arrived, a small man of mean physique, yet he gave the impression of tremendous vitality. A typical Egyptian face, with the large, clear-cut nose and huge, slightly protruding eyes. He was ordinary enough in dissection, yet Mona sensed immediately the reason for Harriet's remarks. There was an atmosphere of evil about him, impossible to describe, yet nevertheless present. Only his hands gave a tangible sign of it, for they were intensely virile, peculiarly repulsive, and withal quite the cruellest hands Mona had ever seen.

It was obvious to the most casual observer that Harriet was fascinated by the Prince, and that she attracted him. Once or twice during dinner Mona saw a look on his face that made her shudder for Harriet's future if she linked it with his. Only Courtley seemed blind to the drama enacted before him, blind with the stupid senseless belief of a man in the inviolability of a woman who has given herself to him in love.

The conversation turned on hypnotism, Courtley relating instances of Irish "blood-healers", those who have the unusual gift of staunching a wound with a few words.

"It is an extraordinary power. Don't you think so, Prince?" asked Mona.

"You Westerns are all the same," he answered. "You refuse to acknowledge the force of willpower. Yet the Eastern nations have developed that force through all the ages. Hypnotism is but the power of a strong will over a weaker. Miracles are performed by exceptional persons who have developed their will until, in the language of the Scriptures, they can remove mountains. Nothing is impossible, nothing unattainable if we have faith in ourselves. Man is a god, but in most cases he is too fearful of himself to realise his divinity. His own worst enemy, he is fearful, cultivating a humble spirit instead of infusing the atmosphere around him with power. Power that, properly directed, will give him all his desires."

"And destroy his soul?" said Mona quietly.

"And what is a soul? Surely an atom of life from life, earthbound for a short space but, with the death of the body, spiritually free. Altered, soiled or damaged, yet still vital, and returning to the inexhaustible source, the ceaselessly turning wheel of life grinding out the generations."

There was silence for a minute. Mona, Harriet, Courtley, all three wondered if there was any truth in this egotistic creed, all thinking of a particular object they desired.

After dinner they were to go to a play. Mona put on her cloak in Harriet's bedroom, an apartment of soft hangings and dim lights. A few of Courtley's belongings were scattered about, giving an air of illicit passion that seemed to please its owner. Harriet would above all things have hated to be thought 'respectable'. She gloried in immorality because it was unlawful.

"What do you think of the Prince?" she asked, touching her mouth with the scarlet tongue of her lip-salve.

"Extraordinarily intelligent, but I think your diagnosis is correct."

"Can you imagine the lasciviousness he would display in his harem?" Harriet's voice seemed to gloat, the raw hungry note quivering.

"Don't!" Mona spoke sharply.

But Harriet's eyes stared at her and beyond they seemed to see a desert of desolation without an oasis.

"I know." The whisper was very low. "But it is inevitable."

For a moment the two women looked at each other, worlds apart, utterly unalike, yet joined for the moment by a vast wordless freemasonry of sympathy. Then Harriet with a nervous movement swept a small bottle from the dressing-table to the floor. It broke, and the sharp noise shattered the tension. The fumes of a heavy perfume filled the room and, with a little gesture of disgust, Harriet threw open a window. The cold frosty night air rushed in, making Mona feel as though the preceding conversation had been a dream.

"Viens, donc!" Harriet wrapped an ermine cloak around her, and without another word, the two women left the room.

The play was a farce, with the usual absurd situations and idiotic bedroom scenes, yet so well acted and staged that almost against her will Mona found herself amused and interested. Harriet was sparkling with levity, laughing light-heartedly as though her path was one strewn with thornless roses. Courtley, engrossed in the woman he loved, was content in her happiness. Only the Prince was a being apart, bored with the performance and apparently engrossed with his own thoughts. Once, during a particularly indecent and obscene apache dance, Harriet glanced back at him over a naked shoulder and Mona, almost unconsciously intercepting her look and his, felt an irrepressible shudder shake her whole being. Passion stared from the black eyes of the Prince, the pupils narrowed, then enlarged hypnotically – passion, fiery and uncurbed, bodily desires portrayed nakedly and unashamed without the softening veil of illusion or the clothing of affection.

Harriet was almost mesmerised, held by a mystic force that made her pulses beat and her throat dry with excitement, two white teeth fastened on her crimson underlip. Then with an obvious effort she turned away, but the long quivering fingers told of pulsating nerves.

So suddenly that Mona jumped, Harriet rose, pushing back her chair until it fell to the ground with a muffled crash. She drew her cloak tightly round her slim figure and from the softness of her fur collar her face gleamed white and strange in the semi-darkness.

"This is so dull." Her low voice seemed to be dragged forcibly through the scarlet mouth, husky from emotion too deep for expression, so concupiscent as to make the commonplace words sound brazen, as though she undressed in public.

Mona rose slowly. She knew breaking point had been reached.

Courtley, vaguely aware of an undercurrent of unrest, touched Harriet's arm.

"You aren't ill, darling?"

As though a snake had stung her, she shook off his hand.

"Ne fais pas ça!"

Courtley, crestfallen as a whipped dog, fell back and Harriet passed through the door, followed by the Prince.

"She is not well." Courtley was speaking more to himself than to Mona.

"I think she is tired." Mona tried to smile as he helped her into het furs. Yet there was a tension in the air, the oppression of a storm was hemming them in.

They walked quickly down the red-carpeted corridors to the wide entrance hall. It was deserted save for the commissionaire and a *fille de joie,* who glanced at Courtley with bold eyes until she espied Mona.

Outside there was no sign of the car. The commissionaire was questioned.

"*Oui,* – a lady and a gentleman had just driven off."

Courtley found a taxi and gave the address of Harriet's flat. They drove in silence, the shrill horn, used frequently by the driver, clearing the way for their rapid progress.

The night porter raised sleepy eyes from a contemplation of a somewhat obscene paper. Madame had not returned yet. For a moment Courtley stood undecided, his face hardening, his hands clenching unconsciously. They re-entered the taxi.

"A hundred and twenty-three *Rue de Republique.*"

Off again, bumping, rattling over the uneven roads.

Mona wondered at Courtley's not suggesting that he should drop her at the Ritz. She was *de trop* but Courtley seemed content with her company, and she dared not rouse him from a moody reverie in the corner of the taxi. There was a lesson to be learnt from this episode in her life, she thought, and realised it to be one that proved the depth of love. Whatever Harriet did, Courtley's love would remain unchanged – hurt, wounded, insulted, but undying, eternal with the divinity of true forgiveness.

"Seventy times seven" was but a phrase. He would condone a million times and be ready to forgive again. And she? Mona accused herself. How could she understand the depth of love with that false spark of pride in her heart which had kept her silent all these months, which had stopped her writing an answer to Peter's letter – an answer that could have explained all and craved his forgiveness. In the wrong, she had refused to acknowledge her fault, merely allowing the breach to continue between them. Peter in all probability still believed her indifference to him was due to her love for Alec. And now it was too late. How could she write after months of silence, and perhaps he no longer cared! Her thoughts were interrupted as the taxi drew up with a jerk.

The night watchman regarded them suspiciously.

"Monsieur le Prince" had not mentioned he was expecting any guests.

So he was here! The crackle of a note and "*Monsieur*" would be pleased to see them. The door of the *appartement* was thrown open. The hall was lit by a red light hung from the ceiling by silver chains and the furnishing was oriental. The airless odour invariably associated with the East was noticeably present. Without pausing, Courtley opened a heavy door and entered a sitting room, Mona following. Low divans and becushioned sofas were empty of occupants.

Suddenly through some heavy curtains drawn across the end of the room appeared the Prince. He had removed his tail coat and was wearing a wonderfully embroidered dressing-gown, a strange incongruity with the stiff shirt and formal collar.

"What a pleasure!" His white teeth gleamed unpleasantly.

Without a word Courtley crossed the room and faced him, speaking sharply.

"Out of my way!"

Beside the great height and broad proportions of the Irishman, the Prince was an unimpressive frippery little figure. Only his eyes held the force of evil.

"You are discourteous, what do you want?" he asked, still barring Courtley's passage.

With a deft movement His Highness was tripped up, measuring his length on the polished floor, his antagonist disappearing through the curtains. Within three seconds Courtley reappeared, half-carrying, half-supporting Harriet, her white cloak wrapped round her, but her hair disarranged and a dazed inanimate look on her face.

Mona held out her hand and Harriet took it, without a word. The action moved her fur round her neck and revealed to Mona's horrified gaze a round crimson mark and the imprint of heavy fingers. Courtley saw it and the Irish blood of generations reddened in his veins.

"Take her home," he said to Mona, and as she nodded he opened the door. The two women passed through and Courtley and the Prince were left alone.

In the taxi Harriet broke down, but her tears were not hysterical like those of a normal woman, but great heaving dry sobs seeming to come from the depths of the fragile body. They shook with their vehemence.

"Hush, dear," Mona quietened her. "You'll make yourself ill."

"Oh God!" The nerves quivered under the white skin. Then Harriet, with an obvious effort at control, turned to face Mona. "You've been wonderfully kind. I pray you will never become like me. I'm mad – mad with intervals of being perfectly normal – like a drunkard between his bouts. Senseless, devastating, remorseless sensuousness! Only Courtley understands and he saves me, fetches me home and treats me as a goddess, when I'm nothing but a..." Her voice broke on the awful word and Mona put her arms round her.

"Oh, my dear, my dear, don't you understand he can forgive everything because he loves you. I never learnt till tonight what true love meant."

"Bless him!" Harriet's voice was very tender, and suddenly Mona found her own cheeks were wet. Harriet had the chance of reparation. Would she be given hers?

CHAPTER XXVI

A fortnight later Harriet and Courtley left Paris for the South and Mona was genuinely sorry to see them go. She liked the bluff, simple Irishman with his great love for the tragic unstable Harriet who, apart from the vicissitudes of her temperament, had many endearing and sweet qualities.

Paris was dull without them, for they had arranged many parties for Mona's amusement and Courtley had introduced her to the English colony in Paris. Most of them were businessmen tied to the Bourse, or diplomatists over for international conferences. Extraordinarily intelligent, with an extensive knowledge of the world, their companionship was not only interesting but an education. But without Courtley's friendly protection and kindly chaperonage, she felt lost and a stranger in a strange land. For these new friends lived in a circle of their own, where all had the same interests and similar ambitions. She had almost decided to return to England when a letter from Sally made up her mind.

Writing apparently in a state of great excitement and hilarious happiness, she announced her engagement to Alec. The wedding was to take place almost immediately because they wished to go abroad, a decision worthy of the impulsive Sally – to arrange a life-contract and to seal and sign it without a moment's serious thought because she wanted to journey *à deux* to the South.

For the first moment Mona thought the marriage entirely unsuitable, all her thoughts for Sally's future happiness. Then, with her usual clearsighted judgment, she realised that the 'new' Sally, the brilliant social butterfly, with her wide knowledge of sex and unsympathetic thoughtless nature, would be the ideal mate for Alec. Both were charming animals with few interests beyond their beautiful bodies, devoid of any sentiment save that of passion. They would fight because each was too self-centred and self-opinionated for domination. Yet it would be the rough-and-tumble battles of small puppies, a moment later the conflict forgotten in the excitement of a new interest. A wife who adored Alec beyond the thought of self would bore Alec before the termination of the honeymoon, but one who could be as indifferent to his word as he to hers, would keep him eternally guessing and at her feet. For supreme egotism, desiring abject conquests and protracted worshippers, will fight till death with bulldog tenacity and never tire until victory is in sight. Alec and Sally were about equal as antagonists and the marriage should last interminably.

Laughing at her own summing up, Mona sent a congratulatory telegram and left for England that night.

A radiant Sally rushed round to South Street next morning.

"Darling, everything is too marvellous," was the principal theme of her conversation, yet it was the material assets that thrilled her the most, the magnificent collection of presents arriving daily, the splendour of Alec's house, car and personal acquirements, the position she would hold as sister-in-law of a Duke, and the tiara she would wear at the next Court. At last, as Sally paused for breath, Mona asked,

"And Alec – you say little of him?"

"Oh, he's a perfect dear about everything, and Pops is delighted with him. My, won't the girls in New York be jealous when I go home!" and that was all Mona could make her say on the subject.

The day of the wedding dawned clear and bright, frost on the ground and sparkling on the roofs. A chill wind made the crowds of pretty women wrap their sables closer about them and ruddy-nosed cabmen slap their arms. About midday the sun shone out and an hour later a ray of multi-coloured sunbeams shone through a stained-glass window in St. Margaret's, Westminster, and lighted the happy face of the bride as she stood beside the flower-decked altar.

The usual overdressed and be-titled crowd filled the pews with their scented, pampered bodies, rustling their silks, patting their dyed hair and surreptitiously powdering their noses, without a thought for the young couple embarking on the new and somewhat precarious craft of married life on to the uncharted sea of the future.

Their whispered comments reached Mona where she sat in the front pew. Beside her was 'Pop' Cutts, proud and pompous with a new dignity, for his daughter was now "My Lady," and his wife, tearful, yet ready to do the honours of the wedding with perfect *sang-froid.*

"Real lace on every garment," she told Mona in an audible whisper as Sally came up the aisle, and Mona turned away to hide an irresistible smile.

The service, with all its solemnity, proceeded without a hitch, the choir sang magnificently and the best man remembered the ring.

The grave words, "Those whom God hath joined together let no man put asunder", united those irresponsible children for all time.

"O perfect Love," sung by the high boy-voices, quietened even the giggling spectators at the back of the church, and

Mona, low on her knees, sent up to a Divine Providence a prayer for Sally that she might be spared the temptations which might wreck her happiness and be guided into the fullness of life without impassable difficulties besetting her path.

A vivid remembrance of her own wedding and the peaceful solemnity of empty pews that fresh summer morning nearly a year ago, made Mona's eyes fill unaccountably with tears. The atmosphere of bygone incidents comes back to us with a sudden vividness when some cord in our memories is touched by our sense of smell or hearing. The scent of lilies and the pulsating music awakened now in Mona the remembrance of her marriage with all the palpitating trembling emotions of when it happened. She felt herself standing before the altar, Peter by her side, his dear face alight with a happiness almost divine, his steady hand pressing her cold fluttering fingers. She had prayed then to be a good wife and a real companion to him and had failed miserably. If the path to hell is paved with good intentions a large proportion of them must be the trusting prayers of the newly married believing in a future where they will live "happy ever after", calling on a distant Providence to remove any boulders from their path that might be dangerous to them or incommoding. The pathetic confidence of human nature, which always imagines the difference of infinite and finite in its own particular case. Dear God! Each marriage is the monotony of thirty villas in a straight row. In the front of each the window is draped with lace curtains, at the back rows of unmended washing, refuse-filled dustbins, an unsavoury smell of cooking issuing from a cracked window.

Mendelssohn's *Wedding March*, containing those magnificent notes of great promise, the chords that herald the culmination of a nuptial miracle, two joined as one, the harmony swelling triumphantly sweeps the united couple down the rose-strewn aisle, arm-in-arm, and drops them in the street of the commonplace!

Sally and Alec sped into their car and the crowd of guests followed. The church emptied rapidly, yet Mona lingered. The lighted altar looked so peaceful, so unperturbed by the pettiness of human nature. Birth, marriage, death, the ever-revolving wheel, whirling onwards through the centuries from space into space.

One of the ushers, a young boy with curly hair and a bright face, touched Mona on the arm. She started slightly.

"May I take you on, Duchess? Sally said I was to look after you. My name is Deresfield, Sidney Deresfield."

"I have heard of you," Mona smiled, and rose to go, with a last look towards the altar. It was as though she left a friend.

As they walked down the red-carpeted aisle, she mentally recalled what she had heard of Sidney Deresfield.

A Canadian, he had taken a scholarship to Christchurch, Oxford, where he had been hailed as the most promising man of his year. The predictions he inspired proved to be correct, for he passed all his examinations with flying colours and there was no doubt that next term he would take his degree with first-class honours. Completely unspoilt, he was nevertheless passing through one of the inevitable stages of the growing man, that of aesthetic cynicism.

Between the ages of eighteen and twenty-three youth loses the faith of its childhood and passes through a transition period when it refuses to accept the experiences of others but has acquired none of its own. Education teaches logic and clear reasoning. Life says, "Take these ideals on faith." "But why" youth asks and denies – not the lack of faith in itself, but the presence of idealism in the world.

Sidney Deresfield was therefore, at the moment, a doubting Thomas, unless he could himself experience the divinity of the Godhead, the ecstasies of the martyred, the beatified transports of the believers who considered the world well lost in the preservation of the soul, he would continue to doubt the actuality of their creeds.

We are born, we live, we die. So much we know to be true, but as to what happens before our advent and after our departure – a gesture conveying nullity would leave his argumentative opponents speechless.

As Mona and Deresfield arrived at the car, a man called Peter Brayton, a contemporary of Sidney's and a friend of Sally's, ran up to them.

"Oh, Duchess," he called out, "I wanted you to come with me."

"And the other disciple did outrun Peter," quoted Sidney slyly, and drove off.

"I think I object to the implication of being a sepulchre," said Mona.

"There is no mention of the words empty or whited," he answered, "although they would be apt descriptions of most of the people who have attended this wedding."

"Thank you for the compliment," Mona laughed, amused at the obviously true implication at the painted affected women and insufferable nincompoops who considered themselves virile men, belonging to a class that, after centuries of sovereignty, is being crushed by the masses over which it has reigned indisputably. Crushed because of bodily indolence and mental inactivity.

The wedding-breakfast, bearing but a shadowy resemblance to the great marriage feasts of the ancient Britons, the six-day ceremonies of the Chinese espousals, the pomp and splendour of the ancient Assyrian nuptials. Yet underneath all their glories perhaps there was as little real genuine feeling as here, in the twentieth century, among the insincere guests of Mrs. Cutts. They kissed Sally and wished her "Godspeed" with as much thought as they wished each other "Good morning". Yet with or without their wishes Sally looked radiantly happy, her white dress and soft veil framing her face and fair curls. She looked like one of Moreau's beautiful statues. Alec was obviously enthralled by her and as he whispered something in her ear she laughed gently and turned impulsively to Mona.

"He is a darling, isn't he, Mona?"

Before Mona could answer Alec had interrupted mockingly,

"Mona, *ma chère*, is proof against all my charms." Then he smiled and Mona realised the venom had gone out of his sting, and she held out her hands.

"Bless you, darlings, and may you find happiness!"

Her voice almost broke on a sob and a moment later she quietly left the house.

CHAPTER XXVII

The old lady who brushes the cobwebs off the stars was plucking her geese over St. Moritz with a vengeance. The few soft snowflakes that had fallen about teatime were now buried beneath many larger brethren. The darkness was thick with them, and they fell against the windows, beating on the panes like frozen fingers craving an entrance.

Peter, Duke of Glenac, looked out of the window with eyes which would have seen nothing at the moment had there been anything to see. He was thinking. With a sigh he drew the heavy curtains. If the snow continued there would be no sports tomorrow.

The last few months had left their mark on Peter's face. The lines were deeper, the grey eyes graver than ever. Through the closed door came the strains of music, the usual after-dinner dance, which would continue until the early hours of the morning. The bright fire, a comfortable armchair, and his pipe seemed to Peter to give better enjoyment than the great draughty ballroom, where the youth and beauty of the hotel danced crazy dances and played rollicking games in which he did not care to join.

On the table he suddenly observed some letters that had escaped his notice. He picked them up and settled himself comfortably before the fire. The first envelope bore an unknown handwriting – Peter hoped it was not a begging letter. He had so many, and it was impossible to assist all. But he hated the refusal even where it was unavoidable.

He opened the flap leisurely, then a knock at the door diverted his attention.

"Come in," he called, and turned his head to see who entered the room. In the doorway stood a vision of golden hair, blue eyes and a dress of soft black lace, veiled so cleverly over flesh pink chiffon that for a horrified second Peter fancied she wore nothing else.

"May I come in?" Her voice was low and curiously sweet. It caressed like the touch of gentle fingers or the pressure of a soft arm.

"Do!" Peter rose courteously to his feet, offering his chair. Mrs. FitzStanley sank back luxuriously against the soft cushions. She was a woman who always relaxed. It accentuated her graceful curves and invariably revealed a good deal of the thin legs that were her most perfect features.

She was a very beautiful woman and blessed with an unusual amount of surface intelligence, which generally assured her success with clever and influential men – the species of game she preferred to hunt. She had also a husband whose habits were universally voted perfection, by envious and less fortunate wives. He was apparently well-to-do, for Ina FitzStanley was clothed in the simple well-cut gowns which women know to be produced by 'Parisian Houses' only. She also invariably occupied a first-floor suite in a first-class hotel, although there was sometimes a whispered rumour of names paying the bills that bore no resemblance to FitzStanley. Another and more important virtue of Ina's husband was that he never appeared. This gave her an inexhaustible subject for the sympathy of her audience, without exception a male one. Her loneliness was a story that brought tears to her eyes and tenderness to the hearts of the attentive listeners.

"Poor little woman," they said afterwards, "she has a damned hard time of it."

At the moment, while Peter was wondering what reason she would give for visiting him in his private sitting room at ten-thirty in the evening and was concocting in his mind an excuse to be left alone, Ina FitzStanley was mentally reviewing what was to be her line of attack at Peter's sensibilities. She had met Peter at a dinner party in London. He had been lonely, his feelings hurt and bruised into a numbness of disillusionment that made him accept the easiest course of action on every occasion, because it was too much trouble to resist. And why should he resist anything? Mona's fidelity had been a fact that he would have staked his life on had he thought of it at all. That the thought never entered his mind was due to a firm conviction that her innocence of passion must remain unaltered until it developed naturally and gave her into his arms. Like many a better man before him he had no understanding of women. That a tiny spark will light a fire large enough to consume a city, was a truth he in no way applied to the incursion of passion. From the first he had had no doubt of her misconduct – his experience with Alec's *affaires* was familiar enough to make that point a certainty.

Broken-hearted but hiding his misery under a habitual reserve, he found Ina FitzStanley an agreeable companion. Not but that he would have forgotten her existence after the first meeting or so, but for the lady's untiring efforts. A Duke, good-looking, rich, and at present unattached, was a valuable asset and Ina never missed her opportunities. But the game was intricate with many unexpected and disconcerting moves. As, for instance, when Peter, taking

Ina to dine at the Embassy Club one night, entered the door to see Mona in a far corner dining with a party. Without a word to Ina, in fact, oblivious of her presence, he left the building, leaving her bewildered and furious but all the more anxious for his capture.

St. Moritz had been her chance – her fair beauty showed to its best advantage against the snowy background, and her figure in boyish garments could not pass unnoticed. She was no mean exponent of the art of ski-ing and the year before had carried off all the prizes for ice-skating. Yet the weeks passed uneventfully and Ina was rapidly nearing the end of her patience. All day she was the untiring companion, at night her dresses revealed truly feminine charms. Yet to Peter she might have been stuffed with sawdust. His courteous considerate manner never changed. He never repulsed Ina's efforts at seduction but remained unaware of their attraction with an indifference that at times made Ina long to strike him. Tonight she meant to end this farce. That Peter had gone straight to his sitting room after dinner had been a move which pleased her considerably. There would be no trouble now in getting him alone. She pouted up at him as he towered over her.

"Peter, you are very unsociable." She called him by his christian name without invitation although he still addressed her formally.

"I'm sorry." He smiled genially, but there were no secrets in his smile for her, no subtle inflection it would not have contained if directed at the merest *gamin* outside.

"I don't think you realise what a lonely evening it means for me if you disappear after dinner." There was a suspicion of a break in Ina's soft voice. Peter began to feel rather uncomfortable. He wished she would state her business and go.

"But I forgive you!" There was a lightning change in Ina's mood. She had noticed the faint annoyance in his eyes. "It is so cosy and homely up here after the racket downstairs. I don't wonder at your preference. Now sit down and be comfortable." She patted a chair beside hers, the movement showing to advantage the shapely white hands with their gleaming pink nails.

Peter sat down wearily. He wondered vaguely who his letters were from and what news there was in the evening paper. There was silence for a moment, then Ina, leaning forward to reveal a little more of her naked shoulder and thinly veiled bosom, touched his arm with a gentle pressure.

"I wonder if you know how much our friendship has meant to me." Her voice was so low that Peter almost had to bend to listen. "When I met you, I was tired of men, disillusioned by their bestiality. My faith had been betrayed, my trust dishonoured. My life lay in ruins at my feet." Ina gave a deep sigh which was half a sob. She was on familiar ground and knew her part thoroughly. "And then into my cheerless lonely existence came the one person who could save me from absolute despair – you, Peter! You saved me from myself, from a degradation worse than death, and I can never thank you enough. You have given me new life, new hope. Yet I would give it all back to spare you one moment's pain." Her voice broke and she hid her eyes in a fragment of lawn and lace.

She had given Peter the cue. The next movement must come from him. Her body swayed perceptibly towards his shoulder. But Peter had evidently no idea what was expected of him. Instead of taking the sobbing Ina into his arms and whispering words of loving sympathy, he merely looked vaguely unhappy and kicked the fire-grate in front of him.

"That's awfully kind of you," he said at last, "but I hope such a desperate sacrifice will be unnecessary. As to our friendship I hope it will always be a firm one. I'm leaving here tomorrow, but I hope we will meet again in London in the near future."

"Leaving tomorrow!" Ina's cultured voice almost rose to a vulgar scream.

"I'm afraid it's imperative." Peter had not realised how imperative it was until this moment. Now he wondered why he had stayed so long.

"Then it is goodbye." Ina rose. She knew defeat when she met it face to face. Humiliated and angry, she could have screamed with fury.

"Goodbye." Peter shook her hand heartily. Was she really going at last?

"Why don't you kiss me, you fool?" Ina's upturned mouth and half-closed eyes shouted at him, but Peter merely thought she looked tired.

Sleepy, poor little woman! Perhaps he had been unsympathetic. The door shut behind her with a bang and Ina FitzStanley vented her rage on her unfortunate maid. Two months' hard work and not even her hotel bill paid! The whole thing was maddening.

Peter alone at last picked up his papers and half-forgotten letters. The one he had opened had the address of a very well-known hotel at Cannes and it was signed 'Sally Gordon'.

'Thanks for their wedding-present,' Peter thought and commenced to read. To his surprise it made no mention of the substantial cheque.

'Most estimable brother-in-law,' it commenced. *'This is a letter strictly between us on a subject that must never reach the ears of Alec. Having been married to him for a fortnight, I have discovered a certain number of interesting facts about his past – especially the details of a little affair that concerns yourself. Never being able to force Mona's confidence, and judging by outward appearances only, I believed the worst had happened and you had discovered them. Do you know that Alec only kissed her perhaps half a dozen times in all and very mildly at that? If you do know, you're a fool and a stupid fool, but I give you the credit for believing the same as myself. I swear to you this is true, and for God's sake go and see the poor child by return. She is eating her heart out in London, with never a hope of explanation, and that resentful Scottish temperament of yours confines her to a living hell.*

Yours,

Sally Gordon.'

Peter read the letter again before he grasped it thoroughly. Then, when he raised his head, it was as if ten years had been lifted from his smiling face. Mona had been innocent after all – innocent and deceived by the first stirrings of passion into an infatuation that had threatened to destroy her whole happiness. What a fool he had been! He ought to have understood, to have realised in those first weeks of development that she was trying to stretch her wings. And he, blinded by contentment, had thought her still a child. He was the most to blame, because experience should have taught him the danger of the woman in his wife finding an incomplete lover in him. He would go back to her now, crave her forgiveness and teach her the true meaning of love. Perhaps in time she would learn to care for him, but even their old sweet friendship would be paradise after the loneliness of these months without her.

"Eating her heart out in London." He could be with her in two days. Then he reconsidered. They had better meet on mutual ground. He was the one to ask forgiveness and he would not start by forcing his way into her house. He would go straight to Taylsea and ask her to meet him there. A night alone among the old associations would steady his nerves. For he was trembling now like an embarrassed schoolboy. Mona! *Mona!* How he wanted her!

CHAPTER XXVIII

The Times, most estimable of papers, announced the arrival of the Duke of Glenac at the Grand Hotel, St. Moritz, and made Mona miserably envious.

Lucky Peter, loving every moment in the invigorating air, the bob-sleighing, ski-ing, the unrivalled excitement of the Cresta run, and the social interactions on the ice-rink. Depressed and indescribably lonely, she decided to go down to the country. A few weeks at Taylsea Court would do her good and Togs was evidently pining for freedom. He hated the restriction of his walks on a lead.

They arrived at Taylsea about teatime and it was a homecoming after many weary months. The servants and tenants welcomed her joyfully. They were devoted to the beautiful chatelaine, but they saw a sad change from the bright young bride of a year ago, in the quiet woman who returned to them, gracious with a gentle dignity, yet with a new reserve which refused sympathy and denied commiseration.

The countryside was very beautiful, silvered with frost, which encrusted the fir trees and sparkled like diamonds on the scrubs and sloping banks of the river.

After the excitement of Paris and of Sally's wedding, the quiet days were beneficial mentally and physically. The long walks with Togs in the sharp air brought the colour to Mona's pale cheeks. The long evenings spent reading an interesting book in front of the huge log fires were intellectually propitious.

Various neighbours came to call but, when possible, Mona avoided them. She shrank from their barely concealed curiosity, for she did not under-estimate the interest the scandalmongers would take in her matrimonial troubles. Always sensitive, she now became morbidly so, fanciful and exaggerated. Watching the days pass in monotonous uneventfulness, letting even the hope that had flamed so bravely die from lack of nourishment.

Only her facial beauty remained unchanged, even improved. For it became more spiritual as the youthful contours of her face sharpened, and what before had been a surface illusion was now a definite materialisation of the inner character.

There was little news of her relatives. Her mother, with her usual round of social frivolities, was too busy to write, and Charles, whose correspondence consisted in answering the invitations he desired to accept was, from various reports, engaged in the pursuit of a moneyed widow. Sir Bernard, when he remembered his daughter's existence, sent her a cheerful telegram, but there was little comfort to be derived from the stilted sentences that contained so little matter of real importance.

For the rest of the world Mona depended on the illustrated papers, wherein her friends and acquaintances were faithfully depicted. At Hunt balls posed in stiff early-Victorian groups, at point-to-points shivering with cold and enveloped in furs that revealed but the tip of a frozen nose for the purpose of recognition. And lastly they were photographed in Switzerland, laughing merrily from the debris of an overturned bob or snapped unawares in an undignified position on the ice.

The groups she scanned intently, imagining she recognised Peter among the crowd at a fancy-dress ball or as the last man on a bob, his face hidden.

One day, however, there was no need for imagination. The front page of *The Tatler* reproduced an enlarged snapshot of the Duke of Glenac 'accompanied by a friend', Peter smiling gaily in the brilliant sunshine was carrying his skis and those of a lady with him. Although a fur cap was pulled over her fair curls and a fur collar muffled her to the chin, Mona recognised her immediately as Peter's companion of the theatre.

Madly jealous, she tore the page from the paper and threw it into the fire, as though by the destruction of their pictured faces she could destroy the tie of friendship or perhaps a deeper bond which existed between her Peter and this poisonous woman.

The flames ate up the shiny morsel and as the last fragment crinkled and died Mona had a glimpse of Peter's laughing face.

"Peter, *Peter!*" she sobbed, holding out empty longing arms, but only the mocking wind, howling down the chimney, answered her.

The next few nights she slept badly. Ever before her eyes played pictures of a slim lissom body, fair curls, dancing blue eyes raised to Peter's. She saw them skating, ski-ing, bobbing together, dancing almost cheek to cheek or watching side by side the moon rise over the white snow-clad world – the first stars twinkling, like frozen tears.

Fool, *fool* that she had been! The ashes of illicit passion were very bitter. Surely the Fates had punished her enough, whipped her into a submission, a humility from which all pride had evaporated. She would crawl, barefooted, at Peter's feet now to beg his forgiveness. He had loved her once, but that was a time absolutely forgotten. The little intimacies inseparable from married life, the secrets too sacred to be told save in a whisper under the cover of darkness, the plans for a golden future, were all those as naught under the influence of other eyes, promising other joys, other mysteries?

And the times she had repulsed him, finding his caress boring, hurting him by her coldness, moments that now returned like evil ghosts laughing at her misery. No torture is more vehement than the self-torture of wasted opportunities. Hours of happiness – gone beyond recall.

Yet even mental agony has a breaking-point, when the pain becomes dulled and nerveless. After several sleepless nights Mona was worn out and when a telegram arrived at the Court to announce Peter's arrival the same evening, her senses were almost too numb for her to comprehend the message on the slip of pink paper. All she realised was that she was unprepared. She could not face Peter yet. And this strange new jealousy in her heart bade her give him time to forget the arms he had so lately left. Suddenly, panic-stricken, she sought an escape not only from him but from herself in his presence. A love that at the mere thought of him almost suffocated her with intensity, would rob her of all self-possession if she met him face to face. As these thoughts raced through her brain and the blood drained away from her cheeks, she remembered the butler still waited an answer and in the fraction of a second she made her decision.

"His Grace will be arriving late this evening. Please see that the west wing is prepared and, Macnab, he is on no account to be informed of my presence in the house. Please see that the other servants are warned. I shall leave for London tomorrow morning."

"Very good, your Grace." Not a suspicion of the surprise he felt showed on Macnab's face as he left the room.

Peter was coming home, he would be within a few yards of her, but she could not, *must not*, meet him. If she could but know his feelings towards her now – but she was only conscious of her own passionate longing. A desire so strong, so unruly, that it frightened her.

Not knowing the hour of Peter's arrival, she retired to her room as soon as her lonely dinner was over. With no idea of sleeping she went to bed, but the strain of the past nights and the tumultuous emotion of the day had tired her more than she realised. Like a child she slept as soon as her head touched the pillow, falling into a heavy dreamless slumber. She awoke with a start and was instantly wide awake, convinced that something was about to happen. The room was quite dark and still, but Mona lay listening, her heart beating unaccountably fast. Then down the passage outside her room came slow footsteps.

'The servants turning out the lights,' she thought, and laughed at her fears. But her heart raced on again, for a hand turned the handle of her door. It swung slowly open. Paralysed with fear, Mona shrank back into the darkness of the great bed, the heavy curtains for the moment concealing the intruder. Wild thoughts chased through her mind. Then a man's figure crossed the room, walking quietly but without stealth. He went straight to the window and drew aside one of the curtains. Mona's heart stopped for a palpitating moment, then leapt until it seemed to beat in her throat, choking her. For, standing looking out on the moonlit night, was Peter.

How long he stood there she never knew. The moon cast strange shadows into the room but his back was towards her, his face hidden.

A vivid remembrance of another night came to Mona, and it seemed as though the intuition of her love told her that Peter remembered it too. A night when they had first come to Taylsea. She had been sad, unaccountably depressed, and after Peter had fallen asleep she had slipped from beside him and, creeping across the room like a slender ghost, had knelt by the open window. It had been summer and, although the moon was not visible, the skies were not very dark and the world beneath had seemed but a deeper reflection. The hills had been shadows in the distance, but watchful as though they listened for strange music. Even as she waited, chilling a little in the night air, Peter had awakened and come to her side. Without a word he had held her tightly, comforting her in his arms. Then, as the first pale flush appeared in the east, Peter had carried her back to bed.

"There is always the dawn, darling," he had said.

"Always the dawn!" Was that to be a prophetic promise? Was the night of misunderstanding over, the day of golden sunshine dawning for them?

Happiness was raising its head in her heart, for Peter's love could not be dead. He had come to her room. Every piece of furniture, the soft silk curtains, the photographs, the tiny knick-knacks lying about, would remind him vividly of their past.

Unaware of her bodily presence he was recalling her spiritually.

At last Peter broke the silence with a deep sigh. He also was feeling the loneliness and the uncertainty of the future.

Barriers are easier to erect than to demolish. Memories of the past had been his company all the evening. His apartment in the west wing had seemed bare and cheerless. Almost unconsciously his feet had guided him to Mona's room. He had not meant to reopen his wounds quite so brutally. But, strangely, he had been soothed. The faint fragrance in the air made the atmosphere vital, as though she were present. It was not the empty frame he had dreaded. A great peace had come to him as he entered.

He turned round and stood transfixed.

The moon shot a shaft of silver light on to the great bed, lighting the carved canopy and silken cover, illuminating a small figure sitting in the centre among the crumpled pillows, watching him wide-eyed. For a moment Peter thought his imagination was playing him tricks. This was but the delusion of a tired brain. Two dark plaits fell on either side of the small face, so pale that it was almost unnatural. Yet the quick rise and fall of the white breasts under the thin lace of her nightdress and the quick intake of her breath through the parted lips told Peter it was no dream, but the living, breathing woman of his thoughts.

"Peter!" The word was whispered so faintly as to be almost inaudible.

"Mona!" Peter stood bewildered. "You are here – I had no idea."

"I did not want you to know, I was leaving tomorrow."

Her voice trembled, and there fell a poignant silence. How could she speak? What could she say?

Months like bars of iron lay between them, days and nights each adding strength to the barrier. Yet it was the Peter she loved and knew, who stood beside her, not the stranger who had cast her out of his life, who had taken from her protection, security.

There was a pain in her breasts, half excitement, half shock – it hurt until she could feel nothing else, and yet in it she felt everything. She wanted to touch him.

"I was coming to you," Peter spoke slowly, almost as if his words were torn from him, "to ask you to forgive me."

"Peter!" Startled incredulity mingled with yearning and longing. She put out her hands.

"Darling, *darling* – my God!" Peter was on his knees beside her, his hands holding hers, his dear head bent, as he rained kisses upon them, kisses which were driving away her misery, her doubts, loneliness, pain. It couldn't be true. Her whole being was trembling, thrilling with love and a great happiness. Was she dreaming? She wanted to speak, to tell him everything, to confess her own sins, but her voice seemed imprisoned in her throat. Peter raised his head and looked at her. There were tears in his eyes.

"I've wanted you so, Mona, my darling, can you ever forgive me, my wife – *mine...*"

Their eyes met. Each was conscious of the flame of love and desire within the other –explanations, words were unnecessary. They *knew*. The moment was so poignant, so holy. This was life, this was happiness – at last they realised the immortal divinity of unity 'one flesh'.

The heavens were open, they could hardly breathe, there seemed as if there could be no climax to this but death. Then humanity broke under the strain. With a sound that was the speech of gods, knowing no language or nationality, Peter took his wife into his arms...

www.ingramcontent.com/pod-product-compliance
Lightning Source LLC
Chambersburg PA
CBHW060610310726
48982CB00003B/506

* 9 7 8 1 7 8 8 6 7 9 0 8 4 *